RELUCTANT DUNGEON

MONSTER HAVEN BOOK 1

J. D. ASTRA

Reluctant Dungeon is a work of fiction. Names, characters, places, and incidents either are the product of the author's imagination or are used fictitiously. Any resemblance to actual persons living or dead, events, or locales is entirely coincidental.

CHAPTER ONE
WYVERNS IN THE
WINDOW BOX

Dollitrice Grandmeir sipped her favorite tea from her favorite cup and surveyed the sprawling garden outside the window of her hut. She was in a foul mood. The icon in the corner of her vision blinked an annoying red again. *Damn this magic from the Heroes' Realm,* Dolli thought to herself and took another swig.

She selected the icon and brought the message into full view:

[Warning: Dungefication Imminent!]

Your personal renown with the Heroes of this land has reached a critical low [5/1000]! This, combined with the decreasing citizen count of your zone, [Little Crossroads], will cause the area to transform into a dungeon. Dungefication will begin when the citizen count drops to [125]. You will have [3] hours to evacuate the town. Dungefication will take approximately [2] minutes to complete when the timer expires. Any inhabitants still within the zone parameters when Dungefication is finished will be transformed into monsters. As Regnant of the zone, you will become the Dungeon Overlord upon transformation.

To prevent this process, increase your renown by offering Hero Quests, or increase the population in your zone.

======

"Hero quests," Dolli mumbled into her teacup, then took a sip. She panned over to the menu that let her call heroes to her aid… more like to her ruin. The single, long-overdue quest looked back at her with annoying urgency. "Complete me!" the quest—Plague in the Crossroads—seemed to yell with silent blinks of gold light.

Dolli's lip curled back as she stared at the names of the heroes who awaited payment for mass murder. Keegan, Gamergrl12, and Jelly-d. Those three stubborn heroes had refused to drop the quest and move on. They'd come screaming at Dolli for a few years, but had eventually forgotten about her, and forgotten the old quest in their log. Dolli couldn't cancel it, since the Hero Magic deemed it was "complete." The only way it would get out of her menu was if the three stubborn heroes dropped it, or she paid them.

Dolli would rather die than pay them for what they did to the people of Little Crossroads. She'd much rather die if it meant sending *all* the heroes back to their realm, but that option wasn't on the tea table. There were no options on the table. Dolli and her village were spiraling into the depths of dungeonhood, and there was nothing that could stop it now.

She frowned and waved her hand through the screen. It disappeared, leaving her with the view of her beautiful garden. A shadow passed overhead, drowning her little forest home in darkness before receding as quickly as it came. She wished her sour mood would retreat as fast, and those stubborn townsfolk, too, but they were dug in like ticks.

So what if Dolli would transform into a monster in a dungeon. At least she'd finally have some peace! Between their hostile treatment of her, the local Blacksmith, Greg, challenging her every year for the "seat of power," and the random visits from Keegan—the angriest of the three murderous heroes—Dolli had had enough.

She wanted nothing more to do with heroes, challenges for the throne, or angry villagers throwing mud wherever she went.

Dolli wanted to live out the rest of whatever life she had left in the cottage she'd built so many years ago. Letting the village transform into a dungeon sounded like a good way to go about it. None of the villagers believed it would happen, so the eventual jest—in three hours' time or so—would be on them.

Greg, the self-declared ruler of Little Crossroads, had told all the people Dolli was *lying*.

Dolli scrunched up her face and mimicked Greg, "That witch's gonna sell the land to some hero's arse when we're all gone, make a fortune off the village we left behind!" Dolli harrumphed and took another sip of her tea. "So what if that's my plan? At least I won't be dead, and they won't be monsters."

The seat of power was tied to Dolli's soul by the cruel magics the heroes brought with them when they burst into their world, Hafheim, the land of a thousand oceans. The only way it could be passed on was if Dolli had a child—fat chance—if she was murdered, or if all the inhabitants moved on, or at least, that's what she'd heard. Even more cruelly, Dolli couldn't concede the challenge for the throne. If anyone challenged her, she had to fight until they conceded or she died. She couldn't ask for mercy, as Greg had.

And she'd always spared him. Why?

Every year he'd come back to kill her, and every time she'd let him go with his life, and his shame. Greg improved little year over year, but he was trying. Maybe she wanted him to surprise her and show up good enough for once…

Dolli smirked and sipped her tea. "Not this year though; the pumpkins are coming in well."

The icon in the corner of her vision flared to life and automatically opened before her.

[Population Update]

Another citizen has departed Little Crossroads, dropping your population to [125].

======

[The Dungefication Process Has Begun!]

You have [2] hours [59] minutes to evacuate the town. If the Citizen Count drops to 0, the Seat of Power will crumble, deactivating this zone and killing the Bound Regnant.

======

Well, that was an interesting complication. It was Dolli's understanding that if the village was empty the title could be passed on or sold, but like all information bought from heroes, it was once again just a lie. Dolli assumed whichever hero had told her this fable would swoop in to claim the land and build a new seat of power as soon as hers was dismantled.

But that wasn't the complication that upset her. Dolli had been hoping the villagers would've pulled their heads from their rears and packed up. She knew there were still two children in town, along with a few broken families left childless by the plague. She didn't want any of them turning into grotesque creatures, forced to battle heroes day in and day out. She had to at least try to get the families to leave.

If only she'd been able to discover the way to close the heroes' portals and banish them from Hafheim, but the Hero Magic proved to be complicated, evading measurement by the tools she knew. Dolli had spent long hours in her hut after the plague incident, noodling on the enigma of heroes. How did they get there? Where did they come from?

It'd been hours in vain. She hadn't discovered anything and had only widened the rift between herself and the townsfolk with her retreat into research. Now, she only had two hours and fifty-five minutes to mend that rift well enough to get them to leave.

Dolli sighed and finished her tea in one big gulp. She was going for her cloak when another shadow zipped across the garden. Dolli scowled curiously, grabbing her walking staff instead. One shadow got a pass, two meant they were circling…

She moved through the garden door and looked up to the sky. There wasn't a cloud in sight, but there was a blot over the sun—two blots.

The gray-scaled wyverns pumped their wings furiously as they descended at landing speeds. Their six-inch rending claws dug into the dirt of her garden when they dropped, sending spurts of pumpkin guts across the yard. She feared what those claws might do to her own gut if she wasn't careful.

Dolli straightened and gripped her staff tighter. "Welcome to my seat of power. The property will soon be for sale—"

"We do not come to buy," the male, clearly marked with red along his gray snout, snarled at Dolli.

Dolli cleared her throat. "Well, I'm not in the mood for dying or killing, so you better just move along."

The male looked to his mate. "I promised you a powerful roost."

The female, nearly five feet longer than him, with radiant opal spots dotting her sides, hissed, "Claim it for me."

The red-snouted wyvern pinned his gaze on Dolli, and suddenly she was grateful for her yearly practice with Greg. The challenge pop-up appeared in her vision with a countdown from five. When the notification disappeared, the battle would begin.

Dolli strained her eyes to see around the obstruction in her view. The wyvern's claws were nestled right in her pumpkin patch, and this little lovebird didn't know who he was dealing with. She checked her Spark pool, what she'd use to cast magic, and grimaced. She'd wasted precious magical abilities on boiling water for her tea and was now down to only 500 Spark. If only she'd known she would be having company today.

The pop-up vanished, and Dolli spent 30 Spark to summon the [Anima] spell. Yellow mist materialized over the garden, and the magic of the potions flowing through the vines of the pumpkins activated in a blink. The plants came alive at her command and roped themselves around the wyvern. He struggled against the strong pull of the pumpkin patch with a glint of surprise that made Dolli grin.

"Concede and I won't kill you—"

A wild screech ripped through the air and distorted Dolli's vision. She winced against the pain, losing concentration on the vines as her health bar dipped to ninety percent in the corner of her vision. She'd gotten cocky from all that practice with Greg and forgotten what kind of powerful creatures lurked in the world.

The wyvern pumped his wings and ripped free from the vine's hold. Dolli raised her staff, activating [Voxen Shield] around herself and half her cottage. Blue light sprouted from the top of her staff and blanketed her in a shimmering wave that vibrated the air. The beast ripped at the magic, destroying the Spark that held it together with every swipe. Her pool was down to 350 and dropping by 10 with every swipe the creature made. This wasn't a winning strategy.

Dolli stepped back until she crossed the threshold into the cabin—the throne room. She tried to open the Regnant Powers menu, to activate her traps, but a notification bombarded her vision instead.

[Dueling for the Throne]

You cannot take advantage of Throne Room benefits while you are in a duel!

=====

Drat! How had Dolli forgotten that simple rule?

She dismissed the notification and reached for the nearest flask on her counter. She'd been brewing up a strong pest repellant that seemed quite effective against Wendigo, so perhaps the wyverns wouldn't enjoy it either.

Dolli hurled the glass through her shield. It shattered against the wyvern's face, and the creature dropped back with a scream. Dolli deactivated the shield and ran for her cloak on the wall. The fabric folded around her like a blanket of ice, dropping her into the shadows.

The wyvern roared and smashed his way through the back door of the cabin. Pink fluid dripped down his snarling maw as his head snaked through her home.

"I know you're still in here, *witch*," the wyvern snarled.

Dolli held her breath and inched toward the portal stone she'd left on the table next to her rocking chair.

Air whistled through the slits on the wyvern's blood-colored snout. "I smell your fear."

He also smelled bear urine and nightshade blossom, which was undoubtedly saving her life right now. She slid her foot across the dusty wood floor while stretching and reaching with her left hand.

Creeeeak.

The beast smiled. "There you are."

Dolli leaped and the wyvern lunged, but his teeth chomped down off target. The creature's maw snapped tight around Dolli's staff, yanking it from her grasp just as her hand touched the portal stone.

Dolli tumbled into the underbrush two miles west of her home. She came to a stop with a heavy smack against the base of a tree, and the air rushed out of her lungs in an *oof!* Pain needled through her chest, and she gasped for breath. Another agony stabbed from her skull, and warm blood trickled down her temple.

A notification popped up in her double vision, letting her

know she had a mild concussion. As if Dolli couldn't *feel* the concussion. She gritted her teeth through the pain and sat up. After another minute, she wobbled to her feet.

She grabbed the nearest stick and poked around the dirt until she found a soft spot—her stash. The cover came away easily with a swirl of purple magic, revealing food, restoration potions, clothing, and money. She'd never wanted to leave her home in the mountains, but if it meant surviving, she would do it. She could always build another cottage in another forest.

Dolli gave a flick of her fingers to clear the dirt from her belongings and cringed when a negative buzz filled her ear instead. She was completely out of Spark, and regeneration could only happen when she was relaxing.

With a sigh, she plopped down in front of her stash. Slowly, she sorted her items and watched her Spark in the counter bar climb. When it had refilled by a bit over half, the Dungefication timer flared bright red in the corner of her vision: [1:30:00].

With every tick of that clock Dolli's heart grew heavier. If she left those people to become dungeon monsters in a dungeon she'd abandoned, what would happen? Would the wyverns take over? She couldn't condemn those people to a fate so cruel. She had to get them out, as many as she could.

The village was at least an hour's walk from where she was, leaving them just thirty minutes to pack up and go. They wouldn't be able to take much with them, but they would survive.

With that, Dolli steeled her nerves and found a good walking stick. It wasn't her staff, not by a measure and a half, but it would serve as a Spark conduit all the same. She scrawled in the dirt with the end of the stick, channeling Spark through it as she cast [Wayfinder].

The dirt came to life with green light in two rings. An arrow appeared on the outer ring, pointing the way to the village. The inner ring shrank until three hash marks were between it and the point on the outer ring. Drat, it was farther than she'd remembered.

The furious shriek of a distant wyvern drew Dolli's eyes skyward. She pulled her cloak up around her head, slipping into the shadows and getting on her way.

CHAPTER TWO

THE ACCIDENTAL DUNGEON

L ittle Crossroads came into view through the trees as the timer in Dolli's vision hit [0:10:00] with a bright red flare. Her head throbbed from the lingering effects of the concussion. How she wished she'd prepared better for going through the portal. Of course if she was using the *escape portal* she would be leaving in a hurry, and possibly hurt.

She'd left herself only two Advanced Healing potions—which were far less effective on citizens of Hafheim than they were for heroes. She'd poured the first one directly over the purpling skin on her leg and drank the second to speed the effects. Yet it hadn't been enough to dull the throbbing ache in her skull, which grew worse the closer she came to town.

Dolli staggered past a broken wood fence and through a narrow, decrepit alleyway into the village. So many people had left. Those who remained had moved closer to the village center, where the last standing inn, X Marks the Spot, and the smithy sat amid the other run-down and abandoned businesses.

Every breath Dolli drew sent stabs of pain radiating through her chest. She must've just been exhausted from the hike with a concussion, but by the gods if it didn't feel like the town itself was trying to strangle her with each step she took. Had the villagers learned to hex, and booby-trapped the streets?

Unlikely…

Dolli soldiered on until the worn-down "X" over the three-story stone inn came into view.

"You have to get out," Dolli called to the sparsely populated streets.

The townspeople looked at her with disgust and went on about their afternoon business.

Dolli's head throbbed, feeling like an overfilled balloon, but she yelled again, "There's only minutes left. You will turn into monsters!"

"We've heard that one before, witch," a woman in a blue skirt and white bonnet called. Dolli couldn't clearly see her face, but assumed it was Julie Harken, the village nurse and the only one who kept the abandoned church in good repair.

Dolli stumbled toward her, leaning hard into the walking stick. "Ring the bells, get them out. There's only minutes."

"Stay back!" Greg's booming voice made Dolli's head feel like it would pop.

Dolli dropped to one knee under the pressure, and the timer in her vision fell to five minutes. "Please. Get out before it's too late."

"What a pathetic display. Have you really sunk so low?" Greg's voice sounded far off.

"The children," Dolli said.

"The ones you murdered, or some others?" Julie asked, her fjord-land accent as thick as her fury.

Dolli closed her eyes to keep them from popping out of her skull.

"You should kill her now, Greg, while she's weak!" someone shouted from the gathering crowd.

"I've more honor than that!" Greg bellowed.

"What is this?" Rufus declared, jolting Dolli from her painful stupor.

Rufus Kruger owned the inn and ran a small produce shop.

Dolli sold Rufus her pumpkins every fall—except this one—and over time they had developed a sort of friendship. He was the only townsperson who'd shown Dolli an ounce of kindness after the plague, and if anyone would believe her, it was him.

Dolli dragged herself up with the walking stick and reached for Rufus. "Get everyone out. Two minutes."

Rufus stared at her for a beat, then turned to Greg. "She's telling the truth. We need to run."

"You can run. I'm stayin' right here," Julie said defiantly.

The crowd murmured agreement and conversation broke out. Dolli wanted to tell Julie what a horse's arse she was being, but pain overwhelmed her, and she screamed instead. She was ripping at the seams, her very being pulled apart molecule by molecule. Rufus dropped to her side, his voice far off and hazy. Dolli's vision went dark as the timer hit ten seconds.

"Run!" she shrieked as green smoke enveloped her.

The townsfolk screamed in terror and ran, but it was too late. Energy surged through Dolli, blasting her into vapor. The pain ended in an instant, and Dolli looked down on the village of Little Crossroads with morbid curiosity. She hung just over the inn, but was moving up toward dark storm clouds above. She had no body, but retained her thoughts, vision, and hearing.

A new pop-up appeared with a two-minute countdown. The Dungefication Process couldn't be stopped now, not that Dolli cared—she was just green smoke.

"It's really happening! Run!" Greg screamed. Dolli wished she could reach out and slap him for his stubborn ignorance. His lies and conspiracies had trapped the poor people, tying them to Dolli's dungeon forever.

Lightning pierced the sky and smashed into the road at the edge of town, then lingered. It spread spidery legs that reached up into the cloud of green that was Dolli, then back down to the city, encircling them. Dolli watched, helpless, as the Hero Magic did its work to seal their fate.

When the ring of lightning shut them in, the cloud of green

mist descended in a deafening whoosh. The cloud—Dolli herself —wrapped around each citizen with a snake-like embrace, lifting them from the streets. Screams of pain and terror threaded through the gusting wind. She watched from a hundred different eyes as her essence pulled the townsfolk apart, breaking them into clouds of sparkles.

The children screamed for their mothers. Greg begged for mercy as he always did of Dolli. Julie and the other towns-people fought and yelled, trying to free themselves from Dolli's suffocating grasp, which she could not control. But then there was Rufus, who quietly accepted his fate. His body dissolved, as did the others, and Dolli was left alone in a sea of green.

A burst of light filled her vision, whiting everything out until Dolli saw only a pop-up.

[Dungefication Complete]

Congratulations, or perhaps condolences! Your zone [Valley of Between the Mountains: Village of Little Crossroads] has been transformed into a dungeon.

The remaining citizens are selecting their monster forms now, with your zone restrictions of [Mountain | Forest | Plains]. You will be prompted to select your new form below.

You may rename your dungeon at any time before level [6] from the Overlord menu.

Review Overlord Menu? [YES] [NO]

=====

She selected No. She would have plenty of time to review the menu later, and she was certain it couldn't be much more difficult than the Regnant Powers. When the prompt disappeared, she was brought to a new screen that displayed four different creatures, vaguely human, who looked somewhat like her. It was as if

Dolli's *essence* was captured and molded into the creatures hanging in the whiteness before her.

A warning popped out at the bottom of the screen that stated all current magical and non-magical abilities would be lost, and Dolli would start over at level [1] in her new body.

New body.

The words struck Dolli into stillness. She had lived in the same body her whole life, sixty-eight years, and now she would be choosing a new one. It was an opportunity to start fresh—though incredibly annoying that she would have to start fresh. Those wyverns were powerful. Who knew how long it would take Dolli to level up and kick them out? A problem for later, though.

The first option up was a Golem, a rock-skinned creature that towered above the others. As Dolli leveled up, new modifications of the monster would unlock. The first two choices were wildly different. One would transform the rocky skin into sand, allowing the monster to shapeshift. The other modification grew the monster by two feet in each direction, hardening the skin and increasing health stats. But it had low magical affinity. Dolli could never learn to cast the spells she once knew, and would be most reliant on brute force or other non-magical abilities.

Next was a Wendigo, a gangly creature of the forest that could transform into a horned beast like a bipedal elk, or a nymph with a body like a sapling oak. This one had magical affinity, and Dolli kept that in mind—though the Wendigo's first form was horrifying to look upon. Not to mention her cottage was now covered in Wendigo repellant...

Third, a Belgrus. It was a feathered monster with the body of a bear and no magical affinity. At the first transformation it could become more hawk-like, growing long feathers from the arms and slimming down. At this point, it gained magical affinity, but that would be a long time to wait to cast spells again. The second transformation was more beast-like, gaining a longer maw, bigger claws, and a spiked tail. It was certainly ferocious and the least human of the four.

Last was a Wispelle, a smoky creature of light in its first form, with small antlers akin to the Wendigo, clawed hands like the Belgrus, and interesting facial designs that could only be described as sacrificial make-up. The Wispelle could also take simple physical shapes through an activate bonus ability in the passive [Vapor Form].

Dolli thought of that ability and watched as the bright smoke shifted from a bird, to a cat, to a smaller version of herself. The branching forms were hidden from Dolli with a message that stated, "Monster given unique transformations based on play style." Dolli scowled as she reviewed the stats for the strange creature.

The Wispelle started with a whopping thirty-two points in Magic Affinity, twenty in Mental Prowess, five in Agility, and one point each for Stamina, Strength, and Constitution. It had the lowest of low Health points at just fifteen, but the Spark points started at one hundred and seventy.

But Dolli was getting ahead of herself. Did monsters share the same stat purposes with citizens, or heroes for that matter? Would her Spark work the same way? Dolli detested the Hero Magic explanation menus, but knew it was critical to understand just what she would become.

[Stats Guide for Monsters]

Health	What keeps you alive. Lose it all, and you're finished.
Health Regen	Regenerating the stuff that keeps you alive.
Spark	What you cast spells with. Run dry, and you're doomed.
Spark Regen	Regenerating the stuff you cast spells with.
Agility	Affects Movement Speed Bonus, Weapon Critical Strike Chance, Armor Piercing, and Dodge Chance.
Constitution	Affects Health, Health Regen, Spark Regen, and Armor rating.
Magical Affinity	Affects Magical Resistances, Spell Critical Strike Chance, Spark Regen, and Bonus modifiers for Spark Alignments.
Mental Prowess	Affects Spell Damage, Heal Modifiers, Spark Pool depth, and Profession Advancement Speeds.
Stamina	Affects how long and vigorously you can physically exert yourself, Movement Speed Bonus, Inventory Carry Capacity, and Health Regen.
Strength	Affects Melee Attack Damage, Bonus to unarmed striking, Inventory Carry Capacity, Armor Rating, and Armor Piercing.

======

Yes, it was just as degrading and childish as it'd been before. Well, it was a relief to know that it was *mostly* the same. Dolli noticed the "Inventory Carry Capacity" mention, and for the heck of it, she thought of opening an inventory. She'd seen heroes summon objects from thin air by using their inventory, and if her stats now supported that, maybe she had one too.

[Dollitrice Grandmeir – Inventory]

	GP10: 0	GP: 3	CP: 7	BP: 2

=====

Empty, save for some coins. Interesting. Dolli's cloak and robes must've… disintegrated with her body.

But enough of that. Dolli still had a choice to make about her monster type.

She reviewed the Wendigo next. It started with five Magic Affinity, eight Mental Prowess, ten Agility, twenty Stamina, seven Strength, and ten Constitution, with one hundred and ten hit points and ninety Spark points. It was a balanced role, something that would give her even ground to stand on. But was it the right choice?

She'd been a magic user all her life—though magic had

changed significantly with the arrival of the heroes—and that was one thing she didn't want to give up when she started over. Wispelle and Wendigo were the only choices for her. One would give her a good starting point to survive a variety of encounters, the other was wildly skewed toward magic dependency.

Dolli didn't want to be at the mercy of her people to protect her—they wouldn't. She needed to pick Wendigo. Maybe it was the right choice, but there was so much more magical potential to Wispelle!

Dolli knew what she truly wanted. She'd worked her way out of difficult situations within her limitations before, and having only twenty hit points was just another roadblock she'd figure out on her own, as she always had.

Without another thought, Dolli made her choice.

CHAPTER THREE

MISTAKES

The village, strange yet familiar, materialized around Dolli. She could look down again from a single vantage point, and when she did, she saw the ghostly white hand of a child of smoke. Her form swirled and whipped about like it was trying to escape the confines of her mental definition.

She stood and looked at the townsfolk turned monsters around her. Rufus, the innkeeper, had selected Wendigo. She didn't blame him. It was a good choice. Greg, the Blacksmith, had selected Golem, which suited him perfectly, Dolli thought. There was a good distribution of creature types throughout the villagers, even a few other Wispelle, who all appeared to be smoky half-sized versions of their former selves with horror-light designs on their faces that were each unique, and antlers ranging from tiny nubs to towering racks.

Dolli looked down to her feet, which were absent, replaced by a smoky tail. She hovered about two feet above the ground, with her body being about three feet tall.

"Look what you've done to us!" Julie screamed. She'd chosen to become a Wispelle, like Dolli.

The townsfolk, now dungeonfolk, joined Julie in their airing of frustrations. All at once their anger crashed down around Dolli in a tirade of fury. Dolli put her hands to her ears, but the cries of her people were not outside of her, but inside—just as their screams had been when she ripped them apart.

Anger and fear weaved through Dolli's thoughts with the shouts of the monsters. It was as if she was a conduit for their emotions, like her staff was a conduit for Spark. She couldn't escape what they felt or push it away. Their hatred and disgust flowed through her in unending waves.

Dolli turned and commanded her feet to run toward the inn. Though there were no feet to order around, her smoky tail wiggled behind her as she made her way across the main square. She put her hand out to open the door but passed through the gap in the door without even opening it. She pushed forward, and her body seeped through the cracks and pores of the wood.

Inside the inn, the voices of her angry people quieted, but the feeling of anger, the discomfort and disappointment, lingered in her chest. Dolli wiggled her way over to the bar and plopped down on a stool with a puff of air. She hardly felt the wood below her… she hardly felt anything at all.

Dolli turned her hands back and forth, examining the ghostly smoke that was now her body. Never mind her body, what about her stats? She'd been a level forty-three Witch of the Wilds, with advanced alchemy. She opened her new character menu and looked everything over.

[Dollitrice Grandmeir – Monster Character Sheet]

Name	Level	Alignment
Dollitrice Grandmeir	**1**	**Neutral**
Creature Type	Experience Points	Affiliation
Wispelle	**0**	**Little Crossroads**
Health	Health Regen per sec	Carry Capacity LBS
15	**0.54**	**1.5**
Spark	Spark Regen per sec	Movement Speed Bonus
170	**10.81**	**55%**
Agility	Constitution	Magical Affinity
5	**1**	**32**
Mental Prowess	Stamina	Strength
20	**1**	**1**
Melee Damage per sec	Ranged Damage per sec	Spell Damage
1.1	**5.4**	**21.5**
Crit Chance	Dodge Chance	Spell Crit Chance
1.50%	**2.48%**	**16.14%**
Armor Rating	Armor Piercing	Celestial Res.
1.00%	**3.00%**	**16.10%**
Divine Res.	Nature Res.	Nether Res.
16.10%	**16.10%**	**16.10%**

=====

The door to the inn opened and shouts poured in from outside. Dolli closed her menu and turned to see who'd come to berate her this time. Rufus, in his new horrid Wendigo form, held up his hand to stop someone beyond the doorway. Dolli turned her gaze back to the bar, keeping her head low.

"Just give me a minute," he said. His voice was changed, deeper with a hint of immaterial resonance, but it sounded like him.

"Can I get you a drink?" Rufus asked as his hooves clicked and clacked their way toward the bar.

Dolli didn't look up. She couldn't. What would she see in Rufus' eyes? She tried to grab one of the half-full beer mugs from the counter, and her fingers passed right through the wood handle. "I'm not sure I could," she said with a gloomy chuckle.

Rufus poured her a fresh glass anyway, and one for himself.

He set the cup of amber beer in front of her, then leaned against the bar. Dolli looked up at him for the first time.

Skin hung slack around his black-eyes and hollow nose. Antlers like a stag's protruded from each side of his head. Wooly fur covered his arms and shoulders below his tunic. He still had humanoid hands, four fingers and a thumb, but the nail on each fingertip was thick and sharp like a predator's.

Dolli swallowed back guilt. "You're looking well. What's your secret?"

Rufus dipped his head from side to side. "Became a dungeon monster recently. Not really my mug of brew so far, but I'm sure I'll grow into it."

Dolli reached for her cup, but her hand couldn't grip it. Suddenly, she worried about starving to death. She'd been hungry before she set out for the town—damn wyverns had ruined her dinner plans—but now she hardly felt her stomach, or her body. She didn't have a need to drink or eat, though she very much wanted to get drunk.

She dropped her head to the bar. "I wish you would've listened to me."

Rufus slammed his cup down. "And I wish you would've done what you were supposed to have been doin' for the last six years."

She glared up at him. "And what's that?"

Rufus sighed, and though his eyes were horrifying to behold, they were compassionate. "Leadin' us."

For the first four years of her "leadership," Dolli had spent long hours figuring out how to help the people of Little Crossroads. How to make the trade market stronger, attract more kingdoms to use the routes, convince people to set up shop and make a residence there. She'd worked *so* hard for them, and while the village grew, they cared not. Not a single kind word to Dolli for everything she'd done. Then, she messed up bad for the first time, and she was an *inept witch*.

He placed his hand on her wispy one. "You're Overlord now.

It's your job to keep us going, build us up. I know it's been hard the last six years since the… but that's behind us."

"Not for most people," Dolli interjected.

Rufus rolled his eyes. "Well, you hidin' up in your cottage doesn't do much good, does it?"

"I think everyone prefers it that way." Dolli smiled sarcastically.

Rufus growled. "We're a new land now, a dungeon, and things hafta change for the better or we're not going to make it. Take something seriously for once."

"Right," Dolli said, her chest warm with anger.

She'd never wanted the Regnant powers either, but it seemed she was trapped in an eternity of responsibilities she'd never asked for… unless there was some way to turn over the responsibility to someone else!

A single hope sprouted in her mind, and she opened the Overlord menu. She went to the seat of power, and that hope died as she read the rules. They were much the same for Overlords and Dungeons as they had been for Regnants and Kingdoms. She wasn't ready to die yet, so with a sigh, she panned over to "Troop Allocations."

There was a section labeled "Tasks" with a long, *long* list of things that could be done to improve the dungeon fortifications. Everything seemed to come with an XP bonus for the monster who carried out the task. Some of that XP would go back to the dungeon itself to help level it up, and a tiny fraction would go to Dolli upon completion.

"It seems as if I might be able to give out quests to everyone that'll fix things up around here and get us some XP so we can level up."

"Yes, good start. What can I do?" Rufus said with a skin-crawling smile.

"You're surprisingly calm about all this. You look like a horror from a nightmare, just so you know."

"I thought you said I was beautiful," Rufus said with a playful scowl.

They laughed, and for a moment Dolli felt lighter.

Rufus sighed. "When you came to town those months ago and told us about how we'd turn into a dungeon, I thought about leavin'. I built this inn with my boys—"

"Rufus," Dolli interjected, her heart aching.

Rufus quieted her with a hand. "I built this inn with them. Heroes took 'em from me. I figure now we're a dungeon, heroes will be comin' here. It's my chance to even things out. To take where they've taken."

Dolli nodded. She'd longed to summon the heroes from the Plague quest and kill them, but townsfolk couldn't kill heroes. The heroes wicked magic protected them from citizens initiating combat, but not from monsters. Ah, but she was too weak, now. Those murderers would be high level, and who knew if they were still in the realm. Dolli hadn't checked in a long time. All the same, other heroes would be coming, and the townsfolk could exact a bit of retribution for their losses.

With startling clarity that made her feel quite stupid, the words dawned on her.

Heroes would be coming.

They were just one hundred and twenty-five strong—no, strong was not the right term to use. They were all level one. They had nothing going for them, no defenses, no traps, and they were all new to their monster forms.

Dolli opened her Overlord menu and started looking around. It was broken into four fields: Troop Allocation, Dungeon Abilities, Overlord Abilities, and Lifewell—which was grayed out. When Dolli focused on Lifewell, a notification appeared.

[Seat of Power Uncontrolled]

Your Seat of Power [Cottage at the Edge of the Forest] is occupied by another faction. You may not utilize the Lifewell until the

Seat of Power is retaken by your faction. Other abilities, such as dungeon defenses and renaming the dungeon, are also unavailable. You will still be able to give monster tasks, level up the dungeon, and gain new Overlord abilities.

=====

Well, that would need to be remedied quickly. "It seems since there are a couple of wyverns perched on my porch, we don't have access to a few critical things, including the Lifewell."

Rufus choked on his beer. "Wyverns?"

Dolli hummed. "Yes, it seems I've gotten a bit out of practice with dueling. The damned things forced me to use my portal stone, and they're now squatting on the throne."

"What's so important about the Lifewell?" Rufus asked.

Dolli opened her menu and scanned. "It's where we respawn, like heroes do. If the throne is taken by another faction, we can't use it. If we die, we just have to wait until the seat of power is retaken, or we sit in the void for eternity."

"That doesn't sound pleasant."

Dolli tutted. If it meant being left alone for once, it might not be so bad, but she assumed even there she wouldn't get any peace. If only she could've attracted some heroes to take care of the wyverns before they'd transformed into a dungeon.

With a flurry of thought, Dolli opened her menus again. There, buried between her class sheet and the Overlord information, was the isolated island of Hero Quests. Dolli grinned as she looked at the quest she refused to pay out, and the stubborn heroes who refused to drop it.

The Hero Quests menu had been part of the Regnant powers. It seemed because there was still a quest to award, the menu hadn't been spirited away with her body and everything else she'd once been.

The Hero Magic was fallible after all. She was one teensy-tiny step closer to understanding how its magic worked, and that meant she was one step closer to knowing how to undermine it.

The Create New Quest button was still active in the upper-right corner. Dolli nearly shouted with excitement. She wouldn't have to wait for her townsfolk—or rather dungeonfolk—to level up. She could make a quest and get those nasty heroes to take care of the wyverns for them.

With giddy glee, she opened a new quest and wrote out her decree.

"What are you so happy about?" Rufus asked.

Dolli finished writing the quest and closed the menu. "I think I may have just found a way out of this situation, quickly."

Rufus growled. "Quick solutions were what got us into this mess in the first place. When are you going to wake up and do your duty, Dollitrice?"

"I *am* doing my duty as Overlord. I'm getting the seat of power back."

"Are you? Or did ya find some way to get someone else to take care of it?" Rufus asked with a snarl on his frightening face.

Dolli felt a flicker of fear but swallowed it back. It hadn't been the hero quest itself that caused the black mark on the town's history. It had been a few lazy heroes who cared less for the people than for their quest reward.

This quest wouldn't put her people in danger. If the heroes failed, at least they could keep the wyverns busy for a time while Dolli worked on leveling up.

Rufus' stare bored into Dolli. "Well?"

"It's not going to be a problem," Dolli whispered.

The angry shouts outside turned fearful.

Greg's loud voice broke over the noise. "Monster incoming!"

CHAPTER FOUR

HERO ATTACK!

Dolli popped up from her seat with a thought and dashed through the door to the square outside. The townsfolk, all monsters, held tight to one another as they watched the advancing threat. Not the monster—a short, green-skinned creature bloodied and limping—but what pursued it: heroes.

Greg, the Blacksmith turned hulking Golem, stepped into the middle of the road. "That's far enough!"

"Please," the creature gasped in a nasally voice. "Help. Give sanctuary."

A pop-up appeared in Dolli's vision at the creature's request.

[New Recruit]

Boji the level [6] goblin would like to join your dungeon! You have [25] open monster slots.

Accept? [Yes] [No]

======

She'd never imagined a monster would want to join her

dungeon, but with so many open slots and a need to get her town running again, she accepted. Dolli floated her way over to the Blacksmith and placed a smoky hand out to stop him from slaying the goblin in the street. "He's one of us now."

Greg looked down at Dolli with a pinched brow, his black eyes narrowed to slits. "Yer letting this *thing* be among us?"

"Thank you, Overlord." Boji collapsed, and the health bar over his head drained down to zero. Dolli reached down to soothe the poor creature's wounds, but realized she had none of her former abilities. Right. She'd have to find a moment to look the new ones over and study the Overlord menu.

The goblin's skin glowed green, then burst in a shower of sparkles. The glittering cloud drifted up into the sky, then zipped toward Dolli's hut in the woods.

"Hey, where'd that little twerp go? I want that loot." The first hero, a tall man with blond hair and shiny plate mail, stepped into the street, panting. His sword was drawn, and goblin blood dripped down to the hilt.

The second hero, a woman in blue robes, groaned. "You don't have to go after *every single monster* we come across."

The plate-mail hero scowled. "But the loot. Fine, whatever. We're here for a bigger payoff anyway."

The dungeonfolk glanced at each other in confusion.

"Oh, you mean my quest?" Dolli asked as she floated to the front of the crowd.

The lead hero pointed his bloody sword at Dolli. "You? Wait. This is a dungeon?" The heroes turned to one another, and the man asked, "Do you know what happened? I thought this was an NPC town."

The woman in blue robes shrugged. "No idea."

"We're here to, uh, to defeat the wyverns and claim our reward!" the plated hero declared.

"Yes, that's my quest," Dolli said. She opened her menu and saw that the two heroes, JaxAttax and Lillee, had indeed already accepted the quest. Dolli panned over to the Overlord menu one more time just to be sure she wouldn't be breaking any Hero Magic rules.

"Until the seat of power is retaken by *your faction.*" Dolli eyed the words with frustration. Right. The heroes were her enemies now. If they killed the wyverns it wouldn't count as her retaking the seat of power even though she'd given them the quest.

Dolli would have to kill the heroes to take the seat of power from them, and if they left—as they usually did in a conjured portal as soon as their work was done—she'd never be able to get the seat back, and never be able to progress the town. What a predicament she was in now.

"*Hellooo?*" the robed hero asked in an annoying tone. "Where are these wyverns? I want an egg for my collection."

"Oh, well they're nearby," Dolli said. She didn't know how much longer she could stall, but she needed a look at her abilities. Blast, why hadn't she looked at her abilities when she was in the bar!

Dolli opened the Wispelle tab and quickly scanned the top of the spell tree.

[Dollitrice Grandmeir – Monster Ability Sheet]

Wispelle Spells and Abilities			
Unclaimed Ability Points: 1	Undiscovered Information	Undiscovered Information	Undiscovered Information
Nature	**Celestial**	**Divine**	**Nether**
Vapor Form (1)	Spark Lance	Zeal	Leech
|	|	|	|
?	?	?	?

=====

There was one spell already owned—[Vapor Form]—and three she could apply her single point into.

[Wispelle Ability: VAPOR FORM]

Spell type: Passive, Innate Wispelle
Cost: None
Spark Alignment: Nature
Description: You are made of a fine Spark mist and lack real corporeal substance.
Effects:

- You may pass through porous barriers.
- Physical weapons deal 10x less damage.
- You're 10x more vulnerable to magic.

[Vapor Conversion]: Cut your Spark pool in half and convert it into solid matter, gaining corporeal form of your choice. Your hit points increase by [5] for every [1] Spark you convert. Duration: Indefinite.

======

[Wispelle Ability: LEECH]

Spell type: Active
Cost: 10 Spark
Cast time: 1 second
Cooldown: 1 minute
Duration: 15 seconds
Range: 10 feet
Target: Any but Self
Spark Alignment: Nether
Description: You're made of Spark, and the more you have the better off you'll be.

Effects:

- Drain 1% Spark from your target every second.
- Allow your Spark pool to overflow for fifteen seconds, increasing the size by 10%.

=====

"This is getting pretty lame. Where are they?" the plated hero asked.

Dolli ignored the hero and scanned the abilities even faster.

[Wispelle Ability: SPARK LANCE]

Spell type: Active
Cost: 80 Spark
Cast time: 3 seconds
Cooldown: N/A
Duration: N/A
Range: 50 feet
Target: Any
Spark Alignment: Celestial
Description: Fire a lance of pure Spark energy at your target. This energy is neutral.
Effects:

- Spear your target for 2x your Mental Prowess.
- If your Spark Lance kills the target, absorb 10% of their remaining Spark.

Modification: Spend an additional 25 Spark to apply a different Spark Alignment to the Lance.
Disclaimer: Beware of Friendly Fire!

=====

The plated hero growled in anger. "Whatever, man, we can find 'em ourselves. Let's waste these guys. They took my gobby loot!"

Dolli snapped her menu shut just in time to see the plated hero charge forward, sword raised. She ducked low under his swing, and the hero's sword lodged in Greg's rocky leg. The hero jerked on his weapon, but it wouldn't come free.

"That was a mistake." Greg kicked the hero in the chest, sending him reeling backwards.

Dolli opened her menu again and dropped her single point into [Spark Lance]. She didn't know what the fourth spell was, but it didn't matter. [Spark Lance] would do for now.

She fired the first colorless lance into the plated hero's face, earning a critical strike and dealing a significant blow to the red hit point bar above his head.

The robed woman stepped back, her hands glowing a frosty blue. The air around Dolli chilled and her body grew heavy. She dropped a foot, her smoky tail dragging on the cobblestone street.

The other dungeonfolk joined the fight. Wendigos cast creeping moss that wrapped the heroes in place. Lances flew from tiny Wispelle. Golems pummeled the ground and threw stones. Belgruses slashed with sharp claws, rending flesh where they could.

It was a chaotic massacre.

Some lances went wide, bursting Golem arms from their sockets or cracking building foundations. Belgruses' claws ripped through Wendigo hides. Golem stones smashed the faces of friends and foe alike.

When only the plated hero remained, Dolli called for the fighting to stop. "Step back from him!"

Though feral anger lit their faces, the dungeonfolk did as she commanded for the first time in ages.

Dolli, only half her size since she'd used up much of her Spark, floated over the hero. "Don't ever come back."

The hero smiled a bloody-toothed grin. "Oh, I'm coming back with my whole guild. And when I do, you guys are fu—"

Dolli lanced him through, stealing the last of his life and a bit of his Spark.

Victorious, the dungeonfolk cheered and roared. They'd never felt so powerful over a hero before, and Dolli felt that elation flowing through her. They'd been wronged, and they'd achieved a tiny bit of vengeance with the temporary deaths of the heroes.

Dolli reached down, and the hero's inventory popped open before her. He was carrying some low-level weapons and a few silver coins. Dolli didn't think she'd have a need for the money, but she wanted to relieve him of everything she could. She emptied his inventory into hers and immediately dropped to the ground.

[Overburdened!]

You are carrying [28 pounds] and your capacity is [5 pounds]. Drop some weight to be able to move again.

=====

Dolli tossed the coins and weapons to the ground, then turned to her dungeonfolk. "Loot the woman too. Take everything she has. We might not need it, but I don't want them having it."

"There've been some casualties," Rufus said as he limped toward Dolli. His leg was mangled from a Belgrus' claw, and he sported a bit of frostbite on his cheek.

"Not to worry. Everyone can be revived!" Dolli said. She expected the dungeonfolk to cheer, but most ignored her.

"Did you hear me? I said we can revive!" she said again.

"Yeah, so do it already," Greg snapped.

Dolli took a sharp inhale. "We can all revive once we retake the seat of power, my cottage."

"You mean the one inhabited by wyverns?" someone asked from the back of the crowd.

The pockets of mumbles in the group turned to loud complaints. Everyone shouted, their anger palpable once more. It seemed the joy from their momentary victory had worn off.

"I didn't want this to happen! I told you all to go!" Dolli yelled as loud as her little Wispelle voice could.

"We can still leave, you know!" a Belgrus said with a growl.

Rufus stood tall and addressed the group. "You've had years to leave and you stayed. If you leave now, you won't get a chance to pay those nasty heroes back for every wrong they've done to us."

The crowd quieted again.

"We have an opportunity to build this dungeon up into something to be feared!" Dolli declared, her miniature voice not doing much for her Overlord presence. "They murdered our families and abandoned us to ruin. Now, heroes will be coming here, and we can show them just how powerful we can be."

"Why should we follow you? Look where you've gotten us so far," Greg said, his arms crossed over his bulky chest.

Dolli took a deep breath, then activated [Vapor Conversion]. When she looked down, she'd grown legs and longer arms, but was still a smoky ghost. It would have to do. She stepped closer to Greg, hands on her hips. "Because I'm the Overlord."

"She can give us quests to improve the town—dungeon," Rufus offered. "It'll give us experience so we can level up and get new abilities. And we have our transformations at level ten."

Dolli nodded. "Who's ready to get to work?"

The dungeonfolk groaned, and Dolli sensed their frustration. They didn't want *her*. They wanted Greg to lead them for some idiotic reason. Greg, who'd told them all to stay because Dolli was lying. Greg, who'd never won a fair fight against Dolli and always begged her to spare him. It was maddening to feel their desires with such stunning clarity—Dolli wondered if they could feel hers too.

"I'm ready!" Rufus said, his voice projecting through the street.

The crowd mumbled and shuffled their feet, but circled around Dolli. They weren't what she wanted, and she wasn't what they wanted, but by the gods, they'd make it work somehow.

CHAPTER FIVE
FORTIFICATIONS

After a few hours of bellyaching, Dolli got everyone in the new dungeon working toward their goals. Greg supplied axes to the Golems to chop wood, then went back to the forge to start crafting weapons and armor. The Wendigos and Belgruses worked on building walls around the main roads into town, though they focused on fortifying the first few blocks of the city instead of the whole thing.

With nothing but hard labor to do, Dolli made most of the Wispelle in the dungeon practice shapeshifting to help carry debris out of town; the others she had gather up personal items and move them into the central protected area. While the Spark-made monsters were powerful in combat, their practical dungeon uses were limited until they shapeshifted, which held true for Dolli, too.

When everyone was smoothly performing their duties, Dolli had the urge to retreat to her hut. She wasn't tired, her body didn't ache, but she was mentally exhausted—something she hadn't experienced in years in her solitary hut at the edge of the forest. Instead of running, she found Rufus at the inn, hammering a new door into place. It was dark, and he worked by the light of a few candles. Dolli's body brightened the area as she approached, turning Rufus' head.

"Hey," she said.

Rufus stopped to wipe a bead of sweat from his unnaturally pale brow. "Almost finished, Overlord."

Dolli winced. "Please, don't call me that. Don't treat me like some… ruler. I was just saying hello."

"Why shouldn't I call you Overlord? You're doing the job, so it's what I should call you."

"Am I? So far I've given out quests and ordered everyone around." Dolli sighed.

Rufus went back to hammering. "That's part of leadership. Giving direction is a thankless but necessary role. There's a lot more to it than that, though. Give me a hand?" Rufus asked, gesturing with his cloven hoof to a nail that had fallen on the ground.

Dolli scooped it up and brought it to his hand.

"Thanks." He smiled and returned to hammering.

Maybe Rufus was right. Dolli was the only one who could give out the dungeon upgrade quests. She was the only one who could access the Dungeon Abilities and award roles—which twisted her imaginary gut into knots.

There was only one role slot open, and the options to fill it were limited to Architect, Blacksmith, and Lieutenant. They were only at Dungeon level 1, but they were getting mighty close to level 2 from all their efforts, which Dolli hoped would open another spot.

Still, she only had one role slot now, and many dungeonfolk to whom she needed to make amends. One choice was obvious enough, and Dolli didn't know why she was dallying...

Fear, she admitted to herself.

Greg hated her—much like the rest of the dungeonfolk—but he was the obvious choice for the Blacksmith role. The benefits would decrease his production times by 15% and increase his conversion efficiency, saving precious metal. He would also get access to new "dungeon style" plans: traps, gates, and the like. They weren't able to mine yet, but they would need to soon if they were going to equip everyone well.

"Ho' there," Greg boomed, pulling Dolli from the menu. He set his wheelbarrow of spare metals down. "How's it coming?"

"Just fine, thanks. Almost finished." Rufus waved his hammer.

Greg leaned side to side as if he were inspecting Rufus' work. "Using a few too many nails, are ya? I'll make you more."

"Thank you." Rufus grinned, and Dolli saw that familiar twinge of annoyance in his dimple.

Greg picked up and headed off. "Let me know if you need help."

When he was out of earshot, Rufus gave Dolli a sarcastic look that said it all.

"Mind if I drop by and do all this? You're usin' up too many nails. Oh yeah, and call me Overlord-to-be, would ya?" Dolli mocked Greg.

Rufus couldn't contain his chuckle but straightened his expression a moment later. "Don't make fun. He's your citizen."

Dolli sighed and they fell quiet. Greg, the man who'd tried to kill her over the last six years, was one of her citizens. She had to figure out how to lead that man, and all the people who supported him.

"What's going on in that glowing bulb of a head?" Rufus asked.

"Oh, just thinking about tea," Dolli lied. "I miss the taste, the feeling of warmth spreading through my stomach, and the sound of a whistling kettle. What do you miss?"

He chuckled. "Recognizing my reflection. But soon I will. We just have to get past this adjustment."

Dolli nodded. Could they get used to this? "I have some rounds to make, quests to give. Holler if you need any more nails."

"Oh, get off it. But really, I'm sure I will need more in an hour or two. Oh..." He paused with a curious expression. "Why aren't we tired?"

Dolli opened her Overlord menu. It'd only been dark for an hour, but he was right, they should've been tired. She panned through the tabs and stopped on the Lifewell page.

[Lifewell – Dungeon Resurrection Spring]

Your seat of power is infused with the energy of the great Lifestream of Hafheim. The Lifestream is a potent source of revitalizing energy that can return monsters from the dead, heal wounds, and cure ailments. The Lifestream can be divided into [4] Slots at Dungeon Level [1], allowing up to [4] monsters to be revived at one time. You can focus the power of the Lifestream into a single Slot, speeding the recovery of a single monster. The Lifewell is always large enough to hold every monster in the dungeon and expands as the dungeon grows. Deceased monsters will stay in the Lifewell until they are prioritized into a Slot infused with the Lifestream.

[Additional Uses]

~ Rest and Recuperation: The monsters do not need to sleep, but after being active for [24] hours, they will need to enter the Lifewell for a minimum of [4] hours or be penalized with an ever-increasing [Exhaustion] debuff. You may recall any number of your monsters to the Lifewell at any time**.

~ Repair and Status Effect Removal: Returning monsters to the Lifewell will increase their regenerative abilities by [25%]. Keeping a monster in the Lifestream for at least [30] minutes will remove all negative status effects, save for [Exhaustion].

**Restrictions: A monster cannot be returned to the Lifewell or Lifestream while in combat. When a monster is returned to the

Lifewell, they cannot be spawned until their health is fully recovered.

======

Dolli hummed with amusement. "Looks like I control all your bedtimes—but only after we retake my home. We will all need to return to the Lifewell to recuperate every twenty-four hours. We've been monsters for three hours, so by dusk tomorrow we'll need to remove those wyverns."

"We'll figure it out," Rufus said with a terrifying smile of jagged teeth.

"We have to," Dolli added, then turned toward the Blacksmith. Why *her*?

It was a question Dolli had been asking herself since the heroes first arrived and she was decreed the Regnant of Little Cross-roads. Why had the Hero Magic chosen her? She wasn't cut out for this. She didn't want this.

When the inn was out of sight, Dolli slumped against the wall beside her. There was no [Exhausted] debuff yet, but she could already feel it. This was what being a Regnant had been like, except ten times harder, with a hundred times fewer people.

She just wanted to drink tea in her garden again.

"Skulkin' around, just like you did when you was the queen witch." Greg's grating voice worked her nerves.

She looked down the alley to see the tall Golem with the same wheelbarrow full of metal frying pans, kettles, door handles, spigots, and more. Had he been listening to their conversation? Maybe collecting more materials from the build-ings nearby?

"I was thinking, not *skulking*." Dolli crossed her arms and lifted off the ground.

"Coulda fooled me." Greg picked up his wheelbarrow and moved on toward the smithy.

You need to lead this man, Dolli reminded herself. She chased after him, her vapor tail wiggling through the air as she went. "Is there anything I can do to help?"

Greg stopped in his tracks and scowled over his shoulder. "Now you're ready to get involved after we've all turned into monsters. Not when our children were sick and dyin'? Not when the heroes were poisoning our water?"

The light emitted by Dolli's magical body dimmed. "I did try."

"Not hard enough!"

"I did everything in my power. I taught the heroes alchemy. I showed them the way to the plants they needed. I brewed their first potions for them and made their quests. I offered up my equipment—"

"You shoulda done it yourself!" Greg slammed the wheelbarrow down. "How could you trust our fate, my daughter's fate, to body-hopping realm rats?"

Dolli's light shrank further until the alley was lit only by moonlight. "I didn't know this would happen."

"You were lazy. You thought you could pawn off your responsibilities to those heroes and they'd take care of everything *you* shoulda been doing. Curin' us of the plague's not the same thing as collecting firewood, or killin' off some boggarts! That's what heroes are good for, not saving your bloody town!"

Dolli couldn't have gotten any smaller. She wanted to argue back, to tell him how hard it had been for her with a thousand different things gone wrong. It hadn't been just the plague. There were trade reroutes due to the illness and trying to communicate with the other kingdoms, the food shortage from fields going untended, the sudden decrease in treasury capital from the loss of trade, the inability to purchase healers. Dolli had to fix all of that at the same time, and she was only one woman who'd never wanted to be Regnant in the first place!

But his daughter was dead at the hands of the heroes she'd conscripted to solve the problem, and those excuses would mean nothing in comparison. Some of the heroes had made proper potions that saved many of the townsfolk, but some had been careless. They'd mixed the ingredients wrong, whether purposely or by accident Dolli didn't know… and the potions those few had delivered had almost instantly killed the townsfolk who took them.

The distant sounds of axes chopping and hammers driving nails made the silence between them obvious. Dolli couldn't stand it for another moment.

"Do you want my help, or not?" Dolli asked, her light returning.

Greg scoffed. "How are you gonna help?"

"I have a role for you," Dolli said, opening her Overlord menu and going to Dungeon Abilities. On the right side was a column for "Officers and Roles," with a [0/1] at the top. There were the three roles she had available, but only one made sense to give. She selected the Blacksmith role, and a tiny metal pin of a hammer and anvil appeared in the palm of her misty hand.

She held the pin out to him. "I could've just assigned it to you, but I wanted your agreement in taking on this responsibility."

Greg didn't look amused at her passive-aggressive tone, but he reached out for the pin. His stare went blank as he picked it up, and Dolli knew he was reading over the role information.

"It will bind you to the dungeon forever… but there's no one else I'd trust with this," she continued when the silence dragged on.

Greg barked a single, "Ha!" then closed his hand around the pin. "There ain't no one else here who *could* fill the role."

A notification appeared.

[Greggory Ferrier has accepted the role of Blacksmith!]

The Blacksmith role may assign related monster tasks such as collection and deconstruction at level [1]. At level [2], the Blacksmith may take on a single apprentice. At level [5] the Blacksmith may take on two more apprentices and assign additional monster tasks such as assembly and installation. Overlord gains 5% of all blacksmithing-related XP generated by the Blacksmith and their apprentice(s).

======

Dolli looked up at Greg. A soft green glow emanated from his chest where the pin was imbedded into his stone. The magic faded to a soft thrum like a heartbeat. Well, that would be a dead giveaway to invading heroes that Greg was some kind of special creature… Dolli wondered if she had any indicators on her.

Greg puffed up his chest as he said, "This is my home. I'd already planned on stayin' til my dying breath. I've accepted the offer but know that I'm not doin' it for you. This is for the town, these people. You've failed us, Dollitrice."

No heat came to her face with the indignant anger, but a bitter flavor swirled through her being. "Fine, as long as it's getting done. We're going to need more swords and armor if we're to take on the wyverns and revive our people, so you better get to it."

Dolli opened her Overlord menu and assigned fifty more armor tasks to Greg.

He accepted them with a grunt. "Yes, *witch.*"

After making the rounds on the other dungeonfolk, Dolli returned to the inn, the only place she felt welcome—or at least not openly disdained. With the information from the others in mind, she scrawled in the dirt with her tail-tendril made of pure Spark. It'd taken a few hours, but she was starting to get the hang of her new body.

"Carry the two," she mumbled as she calculated the coming battle. As sure as the sun set in the west, Dolli knew in her gut they didn't have enough firepower to take down those wyverns. She was on the verge of leveling up to two and knew several of her dungeonfolk were already three going on four. Still, it'd be like throwing pebbles at a landslide.

"We need more monsters?" Rufus asked as he looked over the dirt drawings.

Dolli nodded. "Even with everyone wearing armor who can, wielding weapons where it helps, and leveled up to six—which is about how far I think we can chance it before we're experiencing the debuff—it won't be enough."

"What are we going to do?"

Dolli looked up toward her mountain cabin and grimaced. "Recruit."

CHAPTER SIX

RECRUITMENT EFFORTS

Morning mist hung over the trees as Dolli, Rufus, and the three new monsters they'd convinced to join the cause walked back to town. Moko, another goblin like Boji, spoke the common tongue, but the other two creatures were a pair of skolf: angry, smelly, non-magic monsters with long black maws full of jagged teeth.

Rufus had soothed them with a few chunks of meat, and when Dolli got the pop-up request that the skolf would join the dungeon, she hastily accepted. They were level eleven and twelve, and while they didn't like to take commands from Dolli since she was so much lower level than them, they could be convinced into action with meat.

They still had twenty-one open dungeon slots, and when the dungeon leveled up to two, it would get five more, along with a host of other benefits. Dolli was hoping there'd be some game-changing upgrades she could give her people. She'd leveled up to two from all the completed quests back in town, and was now on her way to three. She'd have to take a moment when they returned to comb over the new options.

"Much farther?" Moko asked in the nasally growl of a goblin.

"Just a few minutes away," Rufus replied.

Dolli heard the clang of steel on steel in the distance, and though she hoped it was Greg working away at his anvil, she knew in her heart it was another band of heroes.

"We need to pick up the pace, Rufus," Dolli said, darting ahead.

"Trouble, Overlord?" Moko asked, breaking into a jog beside Dolli.

"I hope not."

Screams drifted through the thinning tree line and Dolli put on a burst of speed.

"Too slow," Rufus said, then scooped Dolli up into his long arms. She latched on to an antler as he dropped to all fours and sprinted like the skolf into the village streets.

They emerged from the back alleys to the center crossroad, where six heroes stood over the corpses of two dungeonfolk, and had five more backed into a corner.

Dolli held tight to an antler with one hand and readied a lance in the other. "Rufus, [Creeping Moss]. Moko, grab a blade. Skolf, stand back and wait for my signal!"

She targeted the lowest-health hero and let her lance fly. It landed true, slaying the hero in a burst of bright light. Rufus skidded to a halt when he was in range, then cast his detainment spell. The heroes scrambled about to get equilibrium, pinning their backs to one another as they fought the battle from both ends. The plated asshole from earlier was back, shouting orders to the remaining four.

"Skolf, go get some meat!" Dolli ordered, and the stinky things darted into combat. They were agile and weasel-like, and dodged the heroes' strikes with ease. Dolli launched a lance at their healer, spearing him through the chest and eliciting a cry of agony.

The action had drawn the attention of the whole dungeon, and soon, fifteen monsters descended on the battle.

"Casters, bombard the armored! Melee, charge casters!" Dolli yelled, and the other three Wispelle launched simultaneous lances at the plated jerk. He pulled up a shield that deflected two of the magic spears, but one hit his leg, dropping him to a knee.

"This is stupid! You can't aggro the whole dungeon to take us every time!" the plated hero whined, slashing at a skolf. It darted left, then leapt for the plate gap at his armpit. The hero shrieked as the skolf wiggled into his breastplate through the hole.

Dolli's monsters made quick work of the heroes until only the leader remained, screaming in pain as the skolf ate him from the inside out. Dolli grabbed a dagger from one of the deceased and held it to the flailing hero's neck. "Don't. Come. Back."

She pushed the blade through his throat, cutting his scream short. His eyes focused on her as blood dribbled down his lips. "Yer… dead now… fartcrack."

"No, you're dead," Greg bellowed and brought his hammer down on the hero's face. Blood and bone splattered out from the impact, then all was still and silent. The skolf crawled out from under the hero's breastplate, a chunk of meat dangling from its mouth.

"Is everyone alright?" Dolli asked, scanning her remaining dungeonfolk.

"Not everyone," said Julie, another Wispelle, as she pointed to the dead.

Dolli nodded. "We'll get them back. Take everything you can from these heroes. Magic items come to me for redistribution, money to the stash, metal to Greg for repurposing. Everyone clear?"

"Clear, Overlord," her dungeonfolk replied.

They got to work without complaint. In all, there were ten magical items: four rings, a dagger, a staff, a bow, plate boots from the leader, leather gloves, and the healer's robes. Weapons and armor with no magical affinity piled up in a wheelbarrow for Greg, and Dolli got to work distributing the loot, keeping only an uncommon +2 Stamina +5 Magical Affinity ring for herself.

The bodies of the slain burst into sparkles, her monsters retreating to the Lifewell in her cabin, where they would have to wait indefinitely until Dolli reclaimed the seat of power. The heroes' magical essences took off to the east, toward the large kingdom against the sea and their "respawn points." Much like Dolli's dungeonfolk now, the heroes would bind their essence to a "friendly" seat of power. For a time, some heroes had bound themselves to Dolli's own seat, spending time building up the merchant wing of the village.

Dolli sighed and banished the thoughts. There was no time to waste thinking about the past when there was looting to be done! She took corporeal form and gathered up the money, then dished out another round of dungeon-improvement quests for her monsters.

When all that was finished, she took a moment to breathe and opened her Overlord menu. She was immediately bombarded by back-to-back pop-ups.

[Congratulations – You have achieved Level 5]

Unclaimed Stat Points: [50]
Unclaimed Ability Points: [5]
[5] levels remain until first character modification: [ERR: Options unavailable. Still Calculating Play Style].

======

[Congratulations – Your dungeon has reached Level 2]

Unused Monster Slots: [31/135]
Undistributed Roles: [1/2]
Open Lifestream Slots: [5/5]
Unclaimed Overlord Ability Points: [1]
[3] levels remain until first dungeon ability: Warmonger; Defender.
[4] levels remain until dungeon renaming is locked.

=====

Dolli ignored the level-up menu and focused on the dungeon ability text until additional information appeared. Warmonger would let her send the monsters out in raiding parties and gain a bonus to attack when away from the dungeon. Defenders increased all monsters' health and armor, so long as they were within the dungeon area, and reduced the material requirements for fortifications.

Both were good, but Dolli knew Warmonger was the path she would take for the dungeon upgrade. Waiting around for the heroes to come to her was not her style. She was sick of being at their mercy. She would take the fight to them, wherever they were.

She changed screens to check out the Overlord Abilities. There were only three to choose from at the moment: Dungeon Alert, which would allow her to send a notification to all monsters in her dungeon; Lifewell Enhancement, an overall upgrade that wasn't particularly useful at the moment since they didn't control the Lifewell; and Obey, which was exactly as it sounded. Dolli could turn that ability on, and any dungeonfolk within [3] levels of her had to obey what she said.

Dolli already had a passive Overlord Ability that increased the severity of her "presence" by her level, and while Dolli wished she could get everyone to agree with her courses of action, she was sickened by the idea of *forcing* them. Obey was out of the question, and Lifewell wasn't helpful, so Dungeon Alert got the point.

"Dollitrice?" Greg's gravelly voice broke through her train of thought.

She closed out of her menu, though there was still much to do in there, and looked up at the Blacksmith with a nod. "How can I help?"

He held out two thin metal cuffs. "I made Spark channelers light enough for you to wear."

Dolli accepted the equipment and inspected it.

[Lightweight Spark Channeler of Magical Affinity]

Armor Type: Jewelry
Class: Uncommon
Spark Alignment: Neutral
Effects:

- +4 Magical Affinity
- +2 Mental Prowess
- +1 Stamina

Bonus: Wear two Channelers of the same alignment to decrease Spark costs by 15%.

======

"There's a gem socket that'll letcha change the Spark Alignment when ya want." He pointed to the center of the bands where they clasped together. Indeed, there was a tiny socket on the latch where a gem could be seated.

Greg grumbled. "We'll need some gems first, of course. Mining and all… can't just be stealin' from heroes to fill our needs."

Dolli smiled up at the Golem. "Stealing? I figure it's just taking what we're owed from them, really."

Greg smiled weakly.

Dolli cleared her throat. Obviously, her jokes were still unwanted in town. "This is an excellent addition to our armory. Thank you, Greg. Please make sure every Wispelle is equipped with two."

"They are. These are for you." The Blacksmith turned away, the ground shaking as he went. It was the first real interaction

Dolli had had with Greg that didn't end in him trying to murder her.

The sun peeked over the eastern hills, bathing the village in orange light. Dolli felt a swell of hope and pride as the dungeon-folk got to work on their tasks. They may yet survive and make something of themselves. Not just a town of citizens bending to the wiles of the magical heroes, but a dungeon formidable and independent.

Just as soon as they dealt with those wyverns.

CHAPTER SEVEN

WAR WITH THE WYVERNS

Dolli panted, sending wisps of white Spark into the dusky sky. They'd made dungeon improvements all through the afternoon, getting several of the dungeon-folk—Rufus and Greg included—to level ten for their first transformation. At Dolli's behest, Greg selected Bronzite, the bigger, taller, tankier of the transformations, rather than the Destratos, the shapeshifting sand-stalkers.

It was going to be Greg's job to take any of the hits the wyverns dished out. Being able to turn his skin into solid metal gave him a significant advantage against the wyverns' claws and teeth, making him ideal to be the team's shield.

"Do you need me to carry you?" Rufus asked quietly. He had chosen Stagarth, the more animal transformation to the Oaken-heart's tree-like form. Stagarth offered him good piercing abilities with his massive, razor-sharp rack—piercing power they would need to get through the wyverns' hides.

Dolli took another deep breath and closed her eyes. "No, I can make it."

She couldn't justify using up any Spark to take a more human shape that gave her more Hit Points and Stamina. She needed all her firepower for this battle. Then again, she likely needed all her Stamina for the battle, too.

"On second thought," Dolli said, then reached up for Rufus like a child stretching up toward their mother. Rufus picked her up and plopped her on his shoulder. The view was much clearer from there. Dolli could also hear farther than from on the ground, where the crunching of twigs and leaves dampened other distant sounds.

Her army of dungeonfolk had spread out a few paces through the forest, ensuring that the frontline fighters were higher-level tanks, but there were several rows of them. Fifty had leveled enough to come on the journey. The two children and seventy or so others remained behind to protect and advance the city as well as themselves. They needed to work harder if they were going to be strong enough to fight off the heroes.

They had only thirty minutes until the first [Exhaustion] debuff appeared, and Dolli had no idea what to expect. She'd seen some pitiful debuffs, and some powerful ones in her time. This seemed as though it could be the latter, and she wasn't going to chance it.

"Are you scared?" Rufus asked in a quiet voice.

Dolli felt the fear of the dungeonfolk around her, but that wasn't *hers*. She closed her eyes and quieted the noise, seeking her own thoughts. She was terrified. What if they all died without retaking the seat of power? The potential answers were all too horrible to think.

"No," she finally answered. "I'm confident at least one of us will survive to be the ruling faction at the seat, and then I'll be able to use the Lifewell."

Rufus scoffed. "At least one? That's a low bar."

"I like to manage expectations with realism, not optimism," Dolli said snarkily.

Rufus laughed. "Well, consider my expectations managed."

Without having to watch where she wiggled, Dolli was free to open her Character menu. There had been some difficult choices to make once she'd hit level five, but she was happy with all of them.

[Dollitrice Grandmeir – Monster Ability Sheet]

Wispelle Spells and Abilities			
Unclaimed Ability Points: 0	Undiscovered Information	Undiscovered Information	Undiscovered Information
Nature	**Celestial**	**Divine**	**Nether**
Vapor Form (1)	Spark Lance (1)	Zeal	Leech
|	|	|	|
Symbiosis (1)	Starfire (1)	Mend Wounds	Gravity Well (1)
|	|	|	|
?	?	?	?

======

[Zeal], the fourth spell she hadn't been able to read in time when she was battling heroes, happened to be the best level-one ability—at least for group events such as this.

[Wispelle Ability: ZEAL]

Spell type: Active
Cost: 50 Spark
Cast time: Instant
Cooldown: 10 minutes
Duration: 1 minute
Range: 15 feet
Target: Self or Friendly/Single Target
Spark Alignment: Divine
Description: Empower your target with the essence of Spark to do great things.
Effects:

- Increase target's Agility, Constitution, Stamina, and Strength by 150%.
- Increase target's Mental Prowess and Magic Affinity by 200%.
- Increase target's Armor Rating by 100%.
- Instantly heal the target by 25% of their total health.

Debuff Disclaimer: When Zeal's duration ends, the target is debuffed with the inverse of all the beneficial stat improvement effects for 10 seconds.

======

The debuff was brutal, but hopefully it would all be over by then. With that buff on Greg, his chances of survival shot way up —at least for sixty seconds, which was hopefully long enough for the dungeonfolk to kill the wyverns. He could respawn if they were successful, but if he went down too soon, it would be over for them all.

The next skill she knew would be essential was [Mend Wounds], but it wasn't for Dolli. She had the other two Wispelle get that ability so she could get [Starfire].

[Wispelle Ability: STARFIRE]

Spell type: Active
Cost: 25 Spark
Cast time: 1 second
Cooldown: 5 minutes
Duration: 20 seconds
Range: 50 feet
Radius: 20 feet
Target: Area of Effect
Spark Alignment: Celestial

Description: Rain stars down from on high, punishing all in the area.

Effects:

- Rain down [15]-[22] Spark Stars. Each explodes on impact (indiscriminate) and deals between [6]-[13] +10% of your Mental Prowess in damage.
- Each Spark Star that strikes a living target has a 15% chance to stun the target for 3 seconds.

Disclaimer: Beware of Friendly Fire!

======

An area of effect ability was just what she would need to keep the damage pressure on both wyverns at once. The male would be focused on protecting his roosting female, so any damage done to her would pull his attention—which was exactly what they were going to do. But Dolli would have to be careful *not* to cast it where it could strike Greg, or any of the frontline fighters.

She noticed the numbers in brackets would change based on her stats and her level. There was certainly some kind of "behind the scenes" math happening she couldn't see that was affecting those numbers. More of the Hero Magic exposed. She'd have to delve deeper into that later.

Her third pick, [Gravity Well], was harder to decide on, but she was satisfied in the end.

[Wispelle Ability: GRAVITY WELL]

Spell type: Active
Cost: 50 Spark
Cast time: 2 seconds
Cooldown: 3 minutes
Duration: 15 seconds

Range: 50 feet
Radius: 10 feet
Target: Area of Effect – Discriminatory
Spark Alignment: Nether
Description: Foes within the field are affected by gravity more severely while friends are less affected.
Effects:

- Foes within the Gravity Well will experience reduced Agility, Stamina, Strength, and Movement Speed by 15%.
- Friends within the Gravity Well will experience increased Agility, Stamina, Strength, and Movement speed by 5%.

=====

Another important area of effect that could make or break the coming battle. This would tucker the enraged male out faster, making it that much easier to take him down. Or, that was the hope with that part of the kiting plan.

Finally, though she knew she should've reinforced another spell rather than spend the point on something new, she got [Symbiosis].

[Wispelle Ability: SYMBIOSIS]

Spell type: Passive
Range: 10 feet
Spark Alignment: Nature
Description: Wispelle are emboldened by the presence of their kin!
Effects:

- Increase Magical Affinity and Mental Prowess by 5% if another Wispelle, or Wispelle Transformation, is within 10 feet of you.

======

The first level of the spell only gave a bonus for being near a single Wispelle, but Dolli noticed the level-two version gave an additional 1% bonus for every other Wispelle in range.

"Any Wispelle with a point left, put it in [Symbiosis]. If you have two points, put both in there," she said without closing her menu.

Dolli knew they could never take the wyverns in a fair fight. They would have to put them in the worst situation they could, and gang up on them with their full force. Dolli was grateful that when she transformed into a dungeon the open challenge for her seat of power had disappeared. If Dolli had still been in a challenge with the male... well, it would've been a short fight.

Last, she checked up on her stats. It'd been nonstop work for the last several hours for everyone, and with the leaps in leveling up, her character stats had earned significant boosts.

[Dollitrice Grandmeir – Monster Character Sheet]

Name	Level	Alignment
Dollitrice Grandmeir	5	**Neutral**
Creature Type	Experience Points	Affiliation
Wispelle	35	**Little Crossroads**
Health	Health Regen per sec	Carry Capacity LBS
140	5.50	9
Spark	Spark Regen per sec	Movement Speed Bonus
455	17.08	22%
Agility	Constitution	Magical Affinity
6	10	45
Mental Prowess	Stamina	Strength
30	10	3
Melee Damage per sec	Ranged Damage per sec	Spell Damage
4.1	8.3	41.3
Crit Chance	Dodge Chance	Spell Crit Chance
2.75%	4.54%	23.79%
Armor Rating	Armor Piercing	Celestial Res.
6.50%	4.50%	23.00%
Divine Res.	Nature Res.	Nether Res.
23.00%	23.00%	23.00%

=====

She'd gone up to a whopping one hundred and forty health from just fifteen at level one, so she considered that a win. Her Spark was significantly increased now at four hundred and fifty-five, and she could regenerate it all in just twenty-six seconds when she was out of combat. Her spell damage was up to forty-one point three, and her spell critical strike chance was at just under twenty-four percent. Being a monster had some significant bonuses.

The sounds of distant shouts and a wyvern wail pulled Dolli out of the screens.

"Was that what I think it was?" Rufus asked.

"Yes," Dolli said, fear roiling in her.

She opened the Overlord menu and entered a new message to the raiding party: *Hold. There may be heroes in the clearing. Two Wendigos with stealth scout ahead southeast, two more to the southwest.*

The troops came to an almost instantaneous halt. Dolli had

known the [Dungeon Alert] ability would come in handy and was glad she'd put a point in it when the dungeon leveled to three. She'd told everyone to keep a keen eye out for notifications, which most of the townsfolk had learned to ignore over the years.

Four of the twelve Wendigo broke off and moved into the woods. Within seconds, they disappeared from sight and sound, enveloped in green camouflage. Dolli waited impatiently as the sounds of distant battle raged on.

Finally, two Wendigo returned: Brene and Walden. Brene snuck up to Rufus' side and whispered in a smoky voice, "Party of heroes twenty-five strong with two dead, likely two more by this report."

Brene was the only town guard that hadn't been recalled to the greater Kingdom of Edelbrent back when they were a village of citizens. She hadn't lost her military flare in the slightest with her monstrous transformation.

Dolli nodded to the efficient woman. "Distribution of classes?"

"At least five tanks, several mixed casters, few rangers and fighters. They brought a primarily ranged party," she said with a grin, and Dolli knew exactly what she was thinking.

The tanks would be in close to the wyverns, and healers would be sandwiched between ranged damage dealers at max range to avoid AOEs. There would be few melee capable heroes within range, giving Dolli and the dungeonfolk an almost cruel advantage.

Dolli opened her message system: *Change of plans. Compact in and move with haste. We want to sneak up behind the heroes and take them out when the wyverns are nearly dead. Healers first, then the ranged damage dealers. Three to a hero, watch your friendly fire.*

When the message system closed, Dolli saw all her dungeon-folk go glassy-eyed. Then, they converged on Dolli. They moved quickly through the trees, the sounds of battle growing louder with every step. It was fortunate the battle was loud, for the heroes wouldn't hear anything coming from behind. With luck, the Wyverns wouldn't either and Dolli could reclaim her home.

The dense forest thinned, and in the orange dusk of the night, Dolli could see the male wyvern fighting for his life, his health bar almost drained to zero. A pile of bodies lay at his feet. Several smears of blood from heroes already sent to respawn covered the smashed yard that had once been Dolli's garden. She quickly counted the hero party: sixteen remained.

Two tanks were battling each wyvern, and while the female was better off than the male on hit points, it was obvious she couldn't withstand their carnage.

Sixteen heroes, even hurting heroes, could be too much for Dolli and her dungeonfolk, but two critically injured wyverns wouldn't stand a chance. They had to strike now while the wyverns could still do some damage.

Dolli opened her menu: *Go now!*

All at once, the frontline fighters of Bronzite, Belgrus, and Osorath broke through the trees. Hammers smashed skulls and claws rent the soft flesh of the unguarded heroes. Two of the heroes were down before the group even knew what was happening.

"Ambush! Behind, behind!" a bow-toting ranger screamed to her raid party.

Chaos ensued as the casting began. Dolli threw out [Gravity Well], slowing the back row of heroes from retreating toward their tanks for safety and hastening her fighters. When Rufus came too close to combat, Dolli dropped off and fell back to the group of Wispelle clustered beside two hulking Golems.

[Symbiosis] activated as she came in range, and power surged through her. She cast [Starfire] at a cluster of confused heroes. Brilliant blue and pink spears of pure Spark shot from the sky and landed in the decimated garden with tiny explosions. Not every star hit a good mark, but enough of them landed true that Dolli's vision came alight with red damage numbers.

"Run. Run, little heroes!" one Wispelle taunted.

"Who's the weakling now?" a Golem growled as he tore a robed hero in half.

Dolli let out a chuckle. If they were all going to die, at least they were having some fun before they went to an endless abyss.

A burst of bright yellow lightning shot from one of the heroes into the male wyvern, then bounced into Dolli's advancing dungeonfolk. The collective scream of agony as the spell rippled through the dungeonfolk broke Dolli's concentration and the [Starfire] spell ended.

She gritted her teeth against the pain and closed her eyes. When she looked up, the male wyvern wobbled on his feet. The tank hero thrust her sword up into the creature's neck, and a spray of blood coated her armor.

Dolli's troops stood in shock, looking at the eight front fighters who'd gone down from the lightning attack, Greg among them. Half of the heroes turned back, staring down the stunned dungeonfolk. Dolli wondered how she could've ever thought they could take on a raiding party of high-level heroes, an ache growing in her chest as the futility of their fight sank in.

This was the end for the village of Little Crossroads.

CHAPTER EIGHT

NEW ALLIANCES, OLD ENEMIES

Dolli cast [Gravity Well] on the clustered heroes and watched her Spark bar drop to 25%. She'd only get two more good spells in for this fight, but she would make them count somehow.

Three of the heroes resisted her spell, but the others were held firmly in the effects. Golems and Bronzite charged forward, creating a barrier to the more delicate Wispelle in the back. The Wispelle healing team had worked out a cycle to keep everyone alive, and it was still holding, for now.

The female wyvern shrieked in terror, then beat her wings with a heavy gust of air. "Stay back! You cannot have them!"

When the wyvern clapped her wings again, Dolli could see what she was guarding: her nest. Three shiny eggs the size of a melon sat behind her, nestled in pumpkin guts. Well, at least they'd put her hard gardening work to good use.

"I have to help the wyvern!" Dolli yelled but didn't know if anyone could hear her over the battle.

She broke off from the group, circling around the chaos and through the open window in her house to get to the female. Dolli crept up to the hole made by the male yesterday and eyed the three eggs tucked lovingly into the orange goop.

"I can help you if you'll fight for us!" Dolli yelled to the wyvern.

The winged beast thrashed her tail through the air, uncaring that Dolli's home was in its path. Dolli darted above the swipe and pushed out into the garden. The brutal attack landed with a solid *thunk* against the last remaining hero tank, sending her cartwheeling through the air. Golden light twinkled across the tank's body, and her health bar went from nearly empty to half full. *Damn those healing tanks,* Dolli thought. Heroes got all the overpowered and unfair abilities.

"I can help, but you must agree to join our dungeon!" Dolli screamed at the wyvern, who tilted her head toward Dolli.

"How?" the serpentine monster snarled angrily.

"Join us, save your children!" Dolli shouted. There wasn't time to explain the whole plan.

The wyvern growled as a fiery blast exploded against her chest. She was down to just 20% health and couldn't last.

A pop-up appeared in Dolli's vision.

[New Recruit]

Nubiri the level [34] wyvern has requested to join the dungeon. Because her level far surpasses the average level in the dungeon, she will be brought down to level [18] upon acceptance.

Accept? [Yes] [No]

======

The instant she accepted the join request, Nubiri's health bar dropped to 10%. Dolli cast [Zeal] on the wyvern, improving all her stats and healing her by two hundred hit points, but that wasn't going to be enough.

Dolli opened her Overlord menu in a panic and typed a furious message: Wispelle, *heal the wyvern!*

Nubiri's health dropped to 5%, but then, white sparkles glistened around the massive wyvern. Her health climbed, little by little, despite the onslaught of heroes. Dolli had fifty Spark left and knew just how to use it.

She cast [Starfire] on the biggest cluster of heroes attacking her dungeonfolk and watched the [Stunned] notifications fill up the air while she cackled.

With the heroes' last tank finally down, the wyvern rampaged through the remaining casters stunned by Dolli's [Starfire]. When all the killing was done, and only ten dungeonfolk remained, they collapsed to the ground, all but Nubiri. She stalked back to her nest and looked at Dolli menacingly.

"Why have you done this?" Nubiri asked.

"We need each other. We mourn the loss of your mate with you—"

"You would've killed him yourssself! You brought a war party to do just that," Nubiri snarled and looked over the bodies littering the ground outside Dolli's little forest home.

Dolli took a deep breath. "We mourn his loss nonetheless."

"Liar!" Nubiri reared up, claws poised to attack Dolli.

Rufus rose on shaky legs, but Dolli put a hand out to stop him. "I didn't want to hurt you if you recall. I wanted you to move on."

Nubiri hesitated, her claws retracting a hair.

Dolli took a step closer. "I am a witch of the wilds, of life, growth, and harmony. I wish no ill will on any creature of Hafheim."

"And the heroesss?" Nubiri asked, her tongue hissing behind clenched teeth.

Dolli smirked. "Death to every last one of the bastards."

Heat, righteous and determined, swelled in Dolli's chest. Though weak and hurting, her dungeonfolk cheered. Nubiri lowered back on her haunches, still guarding the eggs.

"Then perhaps I will keep you as pets," Nubiri said, setting her deadly gaze on Dolli.

Dolli made herself a little taller. "These dungeonfolk won't be your pets, nor will I. We are a community of equals."

"Equal!" The wyvern barked a laugh. "There's no such thing. But I will let you believe you are equal, *witch*."

Dolli didn't have time to argue with the wyvern, there was too much to do, so this tentative agreement would serve them. The wyvern would soon come to see things her way, when Dolli was higher level than Nubiri.

Dolli activated her [Vapor Conversion] and made herself a stocky body, good for hauling equipment. "We need to get this loot down to the village for distribution and reclamation."

"And you, *Overlord*"—Rufus stressed the word as he glared up at the wyvern—"need to sit on your throne and start reviving our people."

"Right. You know how to run this. Nubiri, we need you to stay and defend the seat of power. Can you patrol?" Dolli asked, simultaneously sending the job request to her. She wanted to let the wyvern know that though they were equals, Dolli still ran the show.

"Sssilly *witch*." The wyvern hummed a laugh deep in her throat and accepted the quest. Nubiri marched with thudding footfalls around the clearing surrounding the home in the woods. That would do, Dolli supposed. She knew she couldn't get Nubiri to leave eyeshot of her eggs and wasn't going to try.

Dolli looked back at her ruined hut. The rocking chair beside the fireplace sat on its side, the fluffy blankets sprawled across the floor. She walked through glass shards and splintered boards without feeling a twinge of pain in her vaporous feet. Sometimes it was nice being made of pure Spark.

Dolli tugged on the arm of the rocking chair and righted it, then climbed up into the cushioned seat. She opened the Lifewell menu and looked at all the poor dead dungeonfolk waiting to be revived. She prioritized the lowest-level folk, as they would respawn faster, and then selected the [Autofill] option on the menu so she wouldn't have to allocate someone to a Lifestream slot every time one became available.

After that, she moved over to the Overlord Abilities. There on the side sat the two locked options for [Warmonger] and [Defender]. She smiled as she thought of her dungeon party roving across the land, picking off heroes and hero kingdoms. They would have their revenge. They would take down the heroes' oppressive system and set the people of Hafheim free.

She changed back to the unlocked skills and found what she was looking for.

[Lifewell Enhancement]

Spell type: Permanent Enhancement
Description: Whether on the offensive, defensive, or just building your dungeon up, the Lifewell is critical to keeping your monsters healthy and debuff free.
Effects:

- Increase Monster Healing by 10%.
- Decrease daily required Monster Rejuvenation time by [5] minutes per Dungeon Level.
- For every additional [10] minutes spent in the Lifewell past full Monster Rejuvenation, that monster will receive a Rested Experience Bonus of +5% XP for one hour. Stacks three times.

=====

Dolli knew it would eventually be an integral part of their plan to storm the world. By Dungeon level 12, they would've reduced their Rejuvenation time by an hour, and that hour could certainly mean the difference between annihilation and survival. Not to mention, keeping the dungeonfolk in the Lifewell for just an extra thirty minutes would increase their leveling significantly. It was a good option.

When Dolli closed that menu, she noticed she'd leveled up as well. She'd unlocked two new spells she could put points in, and while she knew she would be putting that point in [Gravity Well] or [Starfire], she couldn't help but look at the new ones.

[Wispelle Ability: Dust Devil]

Spell type: Active
Cost: 100 Spark
Cast time: 5 seconds
Cooldown: 5 minutes
Duration: 20 seconds
Range: 100 feet
Radius: 50 feet
Target: Area of Effect
Spark Alignment: Nature
Description: Conjure the winds and sands, whipping them into a fury.
Effects:

- Drain 2% Spark per second from anyone within the Dust Devil. This Spark is not added to your own.
- Deal [4-12] + 5% of your Mental Prowess of damage per second for anyone within the area of effect. Damage dealt at the center of the Dust Devil is lower than the outer rings.

Disclaimer: Beware of Friendly Fire!
AOE Spark drain, weapon accuracy decrease, damage to those not in plate.

=====

It was an interesting ability in that the center of the area of effect was weakest. It could be a good balance against other area of effect spells that punished heroes for clumping up. She could corral them into the center—or push them out of range of one another. It was an interesting spell all around.

[Wispelle Ability: BURST OF SPEED]

Spell type: Active
Cost: 25 Spark
Cast time: Instant
Cooldown: 3 minutes
Duration: 30 seconds
Target: Self
Spark Alignment: Divine
Description: Attune with the natural Spark in the air and power your speed with its essence.
Effects:

- Increase Movement Speed by 50% in vapor form, or by 30% in corporeal form.
- Increase Agility by two times your level.

======

Those were both nice, but Dolli needed to improve on the weapons she already had. She dropped the point into [Gravity Well], increasing its duration and potency by 15% and adding a bonus of speeding allies in the area by 10%. It wasn't a big boost, but little improvements made a difference.

Finally, she spent her stat points into a balanced distribution. One each for Stamina, Agility, Constitution, Mental Prowess, and Magic Affinity. She reviewed her changes.

[Dollitrice Grandmeir – Monster Character Sheet]

Name	Level	Alignment
Dollitrice Grandmeir	**6**	**Neutral**
Creature Type	Experience Points	Affiliation
Wispelle	**35**	**Little Crossroads**
Health	Health Regen per sec	Carry Capacity LBS
170	**6.11**	**10**
Spark	Spark Regen per sec	Movement Speed Bonus
520	**17.86**	**21%**
Agility	Constitution	Magical Affinity
7	**11**	**46**
Mental Prowess	Stamina	Strength
31	**11**	**3**
Melee Damage per sec	Ranged Damage per sec	Spell Damage
4.4	**10.2**	**45.0**
Crit Chance	Dodge Chance	Spell Crit Chance
3.25%	**5.36%**	**24.59%**
Armor Rating	Armor Piercing	Celestial Res.
7.00%	**5.00%**	**23.60%**
Divine Res.	Nature Res.	Nether Res.
23.60%	**23.60%**	**23.60%**

======

With that done, she walked toward the battlefield to see what remained. She stopped when her foot nudged a bit of wood that sounded eerily familiar clattering against the floor of her hut.

Her staff!

Dolli scooped the well-loved walking stick up and inspected the damage. It had been snapped in half, but the orb of channeling sat safely in the notch on the side. She rubbed a thumb over the garnet stone, and it hummed with energy.

She equipped the weapon, getting a little heavier, but not so that she couldn't carry it in her vaporous form. Happy to have her old companion back, she continued out to the work ahead. There was a pile of casters' things amid the bloody grass that looked light enough, so Dolli decided she would carry them to town— and look at them along the way, of course!

There were boots, robes, gloves, and mantles, all too high level for her dungeonfolk to wear yet, but she would stash them safely at the inn for later use. They still needed to declare a proper treasury, but the inn was working for now.

She was just looking over the last item when she arrived at the edge of town. Too quiet. She closed the pop-up description of the item and looked through the narrow alley. It shouldn't be so quiet. There should be dungeonfolk making repairs, or at least a few people patrolling.

Dolli hurried into town, her worry spiking when fear, not hers, but one of her dungeonfolk's, pierced into her chest like a knife. The soft sobs of a child echoed through the alley, and Dolli dropped the gear, hiding it under a few crates before hurrying on in vapor form.

She emerged at X Marks the Spot to find a child Wendigo kneeling at a slain Belgrus' side, tears in his eyes.

"What happened?" Dolli asked as she charged forward.

"Dollitrice Grandmeir." The cocky voice of a hero she knew too well stopped her in her tracks.

She turned to see the Dusk Knight, his black armor glowing with the reflected light of his crimson broadsword. Blood dripped from the blade, and he held Rufus' severed head by the crown of antlers.

The Knight smirked. "So, you're a dungeon now."

CHAPTER NINE

RESPAWN

Dolli put herself between the murderous man and the child frozen in fear on the ground. She gripped her broken staff, pressing her thumb onto the power gem, and spoke casually. "What brings you out to the Crossroads, Keegan Plague Ender?"

"You know goddamn well what brings me." He tossed Rufus' head into the road. It made a wet *splat* that turned Dolli's nonexistent stomach.

Dolli looked at the child behind her. "Run and hide, now!"

When she turned back, the air around Keegan was vibrating with red and black Spark. He dashed forward, covering fifty feet in a blink. Dolli knew this move and tried to dodge, but she was far less than the creature she used to be. Keegan's hands gripped Dolli at the wrist and wispy throat. Magic-infused gauntlets thrummed with angry power, holding her still. Pain seared into Dolli's being where he touched her, and her health bar started to drop one hit point at a time.

"I want my quest reward." Keegan growled the words.

His voice was a demonic baritone that shook Dolli's soul. The child on the ground screamed harder, piercing the air with his terror. Dolli's head ballooned with pressure until she thought it might pop, but she kept her calm.

She smiled despite the pain and her dropping health. "That's never going to happen."

"That's just not fair!" Keegan squeezed her throat and the pressure built behind her eyes. "I did my best. I followed your instructions. The game system said the quest was done, so you owe me my reward!"

She'd never seen him this furious. Keegan wasn't able to hurt Dolli when she was a citizen, at least not without provocation, and Dolli would always let her garden do the hard work when he'd come around.

Now, Dolli was a dungeon Overlord, prey to a hero like Keegan. Prey or not, what he'd done was wrong. "You murdered my people."

"NPCs aren't *people.*" Keegan spat the word like a curse.

Dolli had heard Keegan and other heroes use that term: NPC. She didn't know what it meant, but given the heroes' flagrant disregard for their well-being, she assumed it meant they were considered lesser creatures, as one wouldn't care if they stepped on an ant. Dolli was a witch of the wilds; she cared for all living things no matter their stature.

"You're evil, and I will never reward evil."

Keegan put his sword up to Dolli's chest. It pulsed with murderous desire. "I don't think you understand. I'm going to set up camp in your pathetic little dungeon and spawn kill you and your monsters until I get my reward. So, last chance before I shish kebab you."

Fear knotted her chest, and her head swam, but she couldn't let the people of Little Crossroads down. She wouldn't pay this man for the murder of their families. "I refuse."

Dolli's chest exploded in fiery agony as the magical sword passed through her. She gritted her teeth and cast a [Spark Lance] through Keegan's skull. The magic passed through him like a gust of wind, dealing just ten points of damage.

Keegan grinned. "Not so powerful anymore, are we?"

He flicked his sword hard to the right, sending the impaled Dolli flying. She dropped to the ground next to the wailing Wendigo child, her health bar flashing a critical warning.

She looked down to see the tiny beads of Spark that made up her being dim and turn black, sending a cascading wave of icy death through her chest. She pressed her hands against the wound, but it did nothing to stop the slow draining of her life. Darkness crept in at the edges of her vision and the child's screams sounded far off.

"I'll be waiting for you," Keegan said. He raised his sword over the child, and Dolli's health bar hit zero.

Her view of the world disintegrated in a tinkling of green sparkles, then Dolli was flying away from the horror show Keegan made of her village. She watched his sword slice through the air and a spray of red paint the street. Dolli wanted to claw her way back down there and gouge out his eyes, rend his stomach and spill his guts, poison him, hang him, burn him alive!

She should've fought him the second he spoke. She should've thrown everything she had at him. She should've herded the child to safety. She should've…

The village receded farther and farther in her green sparkling vision until she was dropping through the trees into her cottage. Then, all was black.

It was dark for only a flash, and then Dolli was floating in her cottage. The angle of the sunlight through the broken window told her it was nearing suppertime. She opened her Overlord menu and went to the Lifestream. Her settings of prioritizing the lowest-level monsters still held, and so she'd be spit out before most anyone else. Rufus was almost ready to spawn, and Dolli selected the slot in the Lifestream he occupied.

[Set Spawn Point]

Do you want to set this creature's spawn point to a specific location within your dungeon boundaries?

[Yes] [No]

======

Dolli selected Yes, and an aerial map appeared of the valley between the two mountain ranges. She zoomed in on her cottage and set the spawn marker just outside. With a flourish of green, Dolli's vision returned.

Birds chirped in the windswept trees but the thundering of Nubiri's steps was absent. Dolli looked back at the Overlord menu and found Nubiri in the Lifewell. Dolli's mind's eye came alive with the vision of Nubiri chomping down on Keegan, shaking him like a rag doll. Yes, Dolli would need Nubiri for the coming fight.

She waited for Rufus to finish restoring, then took all five Lifestream slots for the wyvern to significantly speed her resurrection.

Rufus materialized in a shower of green light amid the remnants of carnage that had happened there in the early morning. He screamed, shielding himself for a fraction before coming to his senses. He looked around the clearing, his eyes landing on Dolli.

Rufus' wide eyes and heaving chest morphed to a wrinkled-brow snarl. "Where is he?"

"In town, spawn camping us." Dolli began tidying the broken things around her kitchen for something to do.

"We have to stop him," Rufus said, seething.

Dolli nodded. "Oh, I will."

"No, not *just you*, Dolli." Rufus strode forward, a pleading look in his black eyes.

Dolli saw those eyes dead and hollow, blood dripping from the end of his severed neck. She recoiled, looking away from him. She didn't want that to happen to him again, even if he could respawn. She didn't want that to happen to anyone in her village ever again.

"I know that look on your face," Rufus said in a soft, yet accusing tone. "Don't shut yourself up again. Don't go hiding off in your cottage and leave the village to its own devices. Don't pretend you're separate from us, because you're not. You need us, and we need you."

They needed her like a hole in the head… none of this would be happening if Dolli had just made the plague cure herself all those years ago!

Dolli steeled herself, hiding her emotions and pacing out into the ruined garden. "We're too low level to take Keegan on as a team; we would just get in each other's way. I need the wyvern and a couple of healer Wispelle."

The egg roost was empty. No shell bits or blood, no indication that the babies were killed. Keegan must've stolen them. Good. That would be more than enough fuel to whip Nubiri into a murderous fury.

"If you think that's best, Overlord," Rufus said with a dismissive tone that played on Dolli's last nerve.

Dolli whirled and faced off against the towering Stagarth. "Do you have a better idea?"

"Yes. Revive your people. Move the seat of power and start over somewhere else, somewhere the heroes won't find us."

Dolli scoffed. "You want to run?"

"I want to live!"

The clearing went quiet. No birds or bugs, not even the wind through the trees. Rufus massaged his neck, perhaps remembering the pain of having his head removed.

Rufus started again, softer. "I wanted to kill those bastards who ruined us, but now more than anything I just want us all to be able to live."

Dolli wanted them to live, too, but she couldn't let Keegan win. He needed to pay for what he'd done. He needed to concede.

Keegan hadn't completed the quest, so he didn't deserve a reward. He'd murdered her people and called it salvation, demanding payment. He'd treated them like their lives didn't matter, and Dolli was going to show him how egregious an error he'd made.

Rufus dropped to a knee beside Dolli, bringing his eyes to her level. "Is there anything I can say to change your mind?"

Dolli sighed. "I don't even know if we can move the seat of power outside of the zone limits."

"But we could try," Rufus offered, hopeful.

Dolli shook her head. "If we run, the heroes will find us. Keegan will find us. We have to put an end to him as many times as it takes to secure our safety. If that means we're locked in an eternal battle with him—well, at least it'll be a lot of experience points." She smiled ruefully.

Rufus blew out his cheeks. "Fine. But you need more than a few Wispelle and a wyvern. You need me."

"That eager for another beheading?" Dolli asked, bringing an air of comedy to the grim topic.

"Not gonna happen this time." Rufus rubbed his neck again, and Dolli touched the spot on her chest where Keegan's sword had run her through.

"We're going to make that asshole pay. For your sons." Dolli placed a comforting hand on his knee, for it was all she could reach. Rufus put his hand on hers and smiled.

"So let's go get 'em."

Dolli checked the respawn timer on Nubiri. It was still two more hours, and she needed to get a few Wispelle out of the Lifewell, too. And it couldn't hurt if Dolli could get another level. She was just three away from her own level-ten transformation and couldn't wait to see what power awaited her.

She moved a few things around in the Lifestream and got Julie, one of the other Wispelle, in a slot, then set that slot to prioritize only Wispelle.

"We have three hours to get me another level or two, and we

can't stay here. Keegan will likely roam back up here looking for me."

Rufus nodded thoughtfully, then smiled. "I have just the thing."

"Oh?" Dolli asked.

Rufus grinned deviously. "Hunting."

CHAPTER TEN
REMATCH

Dolli held tight to Rufus' antlers as he sprinted on all fours through the underbrush. Bushes and branches seemed to part at his coming, leaving them unimpeded in their kiting escape.

"Get back here!" one of the miffed heroes yelled. A blue bolt of energy zipped past Dolli's head and shattered against a tree trunk ahead. Ice spread across the bark and down to the ground, making a slick patch directly in their path.

Dolli's Spark had finally regenerated up to half, which was all she'd need to finish these lowbie heroes off. "That's enough!" she called to Rufus.

He leapt over the ice, then rounded the tree, charging back toward the advancing heroes. The caster stopped in his tracks like a stunned deer staring down a predator. Dolli cast [Gravity Well], trapping the two heroes in a slowed reality, and Rufus charged with a burst of yellow light.

Rufus dipped his head, using his sturdy antlers like a battering ram. Dolli jumped and flew twenty feet forward as Rufus slammed into the caster. She turned in midair to watch his antlers pierce the man's chest. The rogue beside them yelped in fear. She disappeared in a puff of smoke, but Dolli knew she was still nearby. Even in the shadows, [Gravity Well] had an effect.

Dolli cast [Starfire] over the whole area. Shooting brilliance rained down from the sky in bursts of color, illuminating the rogue. A star smashed the black-leathered woman to the ground, and Rufus cast his [Creeping Moss], pinning her in place. Dolli ended her with a [Spark Lance], and then smiled as a notification blinked in the corner of her vision.

With the heroes dead and combat complete, she opened the message.

[Congratulations – You have achieved Level 8]

Unclaimed Stat Points: [10]

Unclaimed Ability Points: [2]

[2] levels remain until first character modification. Possible transformations: Arattelle, Celestelle, Flemelle, or Ventrelle.

======

Dolli wanted to understand more about the transformations and how they were being selected, but when she tried to open them, nothing happened. With an impatient sigh, she panned over to her character sheet instead. She needed to endure and have powerful strikes for the coming battle with Keegan, so she dropped three of her stat points into Stamina, three into Constitution, three into Mental Prowess, and one into Magical Affinity.

With that done, she moved over to her skills. There were no new skills unlocked at level eight, but she was happy for the point. She'd got enough offensive abilities and needed some defense. Despite [Dust Devil] being amazing, she didn't think it would help her against Keegan. For one, it was an AOE against one hero, and he was in plate, so the damage modifier wouldn't affect him.

She selected [Burst of Speed] instead and dropped a point

there. If she stayed in her wisp-like form, she'd easily be able to dodge and outrun Keegan—at least for thirty seconds—before it went on a two-minute cooldown. Still, that would be more than enough time to get her to dash out of range and rain [Starfire] down on his head. The last point she decided to save for level ten, when her new form and four new abilities would unlock, or so she'd been told.

[Dollitrice Grandmeir – Monster Ability Sheet]

Wispelle Spells and Abilities			
Unclaimed Ability Points: 1	Undiscovered Information	Undiscovered Information	Undiscovered Information
Nature	**Celestial**	**Divine**	**Nether**
Vapor Form (1)	Spark Lance (1)	Zeal (1)	Leech
|	|	|	|
Symbiosis (1)	Starfire (1)	Mend Wounds	Gravity Well (1)
|	|	|	|
Dust Devil<<<<<	Burst of Speed (1)		>>>>>Dust Devil
|	|	|	|
?	?	?	?

=====

Dolli opened the Overlord menu next and checked the spawn timer. Nubiri was almost done reviving, and four of the healing Wispelle were ready to be deployed. Dolli hated holding them in the Lifewell without releasing them since she knew they were frozen in complete nothingness—no awareness at all. To them, it would feel like a blink of blackness, and they were alive again, when in reality it would've been hours. But she had to hold them there no matter the discomfort it gave her to suspend their existence. It wasn't safe for any of the dungeonfolk to wander around town, and she'd need everyone fresh for the battle.

"We're gettin' pretty damn efficient at that," Rufus said.

"A good thing, too. We'll need to teach the others how to fight like this." Dolli closed her menu and approached the downed caster.

He had some low-level robes with +2 Spark Regeneration, and a necklace with +2 Mental Prowess. Dolli took them both and applied them to her character sheet. Visually, she barely changed. The ghostly robes applied to her frame, leaving her image as pale-blue Spark.

She was almost at max carrying capacity just from the gear she was wearing, but it would be essential to be at the top of her game. With that, she did one final scan of her character sheet to make sure everything was in order.

[Dollitrice Grandmeir – Monster Character Sheet]

Name	Level	Alignment
Dollitrice Grandmeir	**8**	**Neutral**
Creature Type	Experience Points	Affiliation
Wispelle	**35**	**Little Crossroads**
Health	Health Regen per sec	Carry Capacity LBS
248	**7.92**	**12.5**
Spark	Spark Regen per sec	Movement Speed Bonus
644	**7.92**	**18%**
Agility	Constitution	Magical Affinity
7	**14**	**47**
Mental Prowess	Stamina	Strength
36	**14**	**3**
Melee Damage per sec	Ranged Damage per sec	Spell Damage
4.8	**11.2**	**57.6**
Crit Chance	Dodge Chance	Spell Crit Chance
3.75%	**6.19%**	**25.69%**
Armor Rating	Armor Piercing	Celestial Res.
8.50%	**5.00%**	**24.30%**
Divine Res.	Nature Res.	Nether Res.
24.30%	**24.30%**	**24.30%**

=====

Rufus rolled the rogue over and looted everything she had.

The boots popped off her body and onto Rufus' legs. He flexed his feet and tugged on the top of the boot until his sharp hooves poked through the toe of the boot.

He grinned. "Still has the stats when ripped."

"Let's head toward town. It's almost time."

Rufus nodded, the grin wiped from his face. "Do you think he's still there?"

"He promised he would be," Dolli said, reaching up for Rufus.

He picked her up and placed her on his shoulder. "Then we better not keep him waiting."

Rufus dropped to all fours and galloped through the woods. The autumn sun drifted through the yellowing foliage and glistened on the dew-sprinkled pine trees. The scent of decaying leaves filled the air, and though Dolli could only *just* detect it, she reveled in it. The ride was almost enjoyable until Dolli remembered she was sprinting toward her death.

She knew she wasn't the firepower in the coming fight—that was Nubiri. Dolli had to be the bait, and she'd fished enough times to know what happened to the bait.

Rufus slowed as they neared the edge of the village and stood upright once more. "Where do you think he is?"

There was a distant, rhythmic clanking like a wooden spoon on a pot, and then drunken singing.

"I think he's gotten into your reserve."

Rufus growled. "I was saving that for a celebration."

Dolli hopped off his shoulder and floated down toward the ground. She opened the Overlord menu and selected a spawn point right next to her for all four of the available Wispelle.

Julie cowered and covered her head, then looked around her in surprise. "What happened?"

"You died," Dolli said matter-of-factly. "Wanna get some payback?"

Keegan's singing went off-key, and he laughed.

Julie's fearful eyes narrowed to slits, determination setting her body aglow. "Let's crush him."

Another Wispelle nodded eagerly. "What's the plan?" she whispered.

"We're going to drop [Gravity Wells] first, all around the square. You take the north," Dolli said, pointing to Julie, then pointed to the others as she said, "you the south, west, east, and I'll take the center. With our combined power, and five chances, at least one spell should take. Then I'm going to kite and lure him close, get him to use up most of his special abilities. Once he's low on Spark, I unleash the wyvern on him. I'll use [Zeal] on her first. As soon as my [Zeal] is down, we'll follow the same cast order as [Gravity Well], starting with north—Julie. Does that make sense?"

The little Wispelle were nodding, their twisted tails flicking and fists clenching.

"He may kill me, that's okay, but don't let him kill the wyvern —she's our only hope of taking him down."

"How do *we* avoid being taken down?" Julie asked.

The ghost-like dungeon creatures looked to Dolli, their eyes wide.

"Rufus will protect you. Split up if you need to—but don't let Keegan survive."

The memory of Rufus' severed head splat on the ground sent a chill through her. Dolli didn't want anyone else to get hurt, but her dungeonfolk were going to die, sometimes horribly. If she stayed strong, if she just kept doing her best, they would be able to respawn and go on living.

"Dollitrice! Where are you hiding?" The hero's distant call came from the top of the church tower. Then, the bell rang.

It was time.

"Stay several paces behind me, out of sight. Remember your [Gravity Well] location and [Zeal] orders. Pace yourselves and keep the wyvern healed."

The Wispelle nodded again, and fear coursed through Dolli. Something else did, too. A nervous fluttering that felt like the moment before an uncertain thrill. Were her dungeonfolk *excited* to fight Keegan?

The bell tolled again.

"Let's put an end to him," Dolli said with a devilish grin.

The fear melted away as the others smiled and determination swelled.

Dolli wriggled with confidence into the open square at X Marks the Spot and came to a stop at the center.

"There you are!" Keegan yelled with sick glee from the top of the church tower.

The air around him glowed black and Dolli began the cast for [Gravity Well] right in front of her. From the corner of her eye, Dolli saw the other Wispelle glowing as they cast the same purple-hued spell.

Keegan leapt from the church tower, cracking the weathered stone and shaking the bell. He flew toward Dolli sword first, but as his body crossed over the first [Gravity Well], he slowed and dropped to the ground in a rolling tumble. He was so drunk it didn't seem fair, but Dolli reminded herself this wasn't about fairness—it was about survival.

She didn't waste another second, throwing an overpowered [Spark Lance] at the downed Dusk Knight. The white light smashed into his chest armor, dealing a solid sixty points of damage. The health bar above his head dropped a tiny fraction, and Dolli grimaced. Nubiri had her work cut out for her.

Keegan dashed from the ground with a battle cry. The [Gravity Well] slowed him just enough that Dolli could activate [Burst of Speed] and wriggle away. She went north, and turned, still moving backwards, and cast another lance.

"Just give me the quest reward! Why are you being such a butthole?" Keegan roared and chased after Dolli—just as she'd planned.

His sword glowed red, and he sliced it through the air. The deadly magic rippled out from his sword in a wide arc and gained on Dolli. She turned and dashed behind a wall. The magic hit the stone and bounced off. Dolli returned to her kiting with Keegan not far behind.

Something hot and angry grabbed hold of Dolli's tail, pulling her to a stop. She turned to see a black skeletal hand growing out of the ground and clutched around her. Keegan surged forward, sword drawn. Dolli hadn't expected it to be over so quickly.

This was going to hurt.

CHAPTER ELEVEN

IMMOVABLE HERO,
UNSTOPPABLE WYVERN

Keegan soared through the air, the tip of his upraised sword glinting a savage red. She didn't want to die again, but if she had to, to save her people and the village, she supposed it was an alright way to go.

Just before his sword hit home, a trio of [Spark Lances] shot from the alley and speared Keegan. He fell back from the force, interrupting his concentration and dropping his health by 5%. The skeletal hand retreated but Keegan was too fast. He was back on the offensive, and Dolli's [Burst of Speed] was coming to an end. [Creeping Moss] spread across Keegan's armor, slowing him just enough to let Dolli get away.

She dashed with the last of her speed and stamina, trying to stay ahead of him, trying to lure all his best abilities out of him. Get everything on cooldown, take all his Spark, and leave him completely defenseless for their true assault.

"Get over here!" Keegan snarled in his demonic voice, and an oversized glowing red hand protruded from his own outstretched arm. The hand clamped down on Dolli, dragging her back toward the Dusk Knight.

She opened her Overlord menu and selected Nubiri's spawn point: directly behind him.

Keegan's sword ripped a hole in Dolli's shoulder, and she cried out. She closed the menu and looked the hero in the eyes with all the hatred she could muster.

"This ends whenever you want it to." The hero reeked of alcohol and sweat dripped down his tanned brow into his red eyes. He twisted the blade, earning a groan of pain from Dolli, but she suffered through it. Nubiri spawned in a sparkle of green, casting light across the square and turning Keegan's head.

The wyvern wasted no time, whipping her tail forward and smashing the hero. Dolli dropped to the ground, her buoyant Spark turning black and decaying. She reached out, casting [Zeal] on Nubiri.

"He took your children," Dolli said, pointing to Keegan.

The drunken hero stumbled to his feet, his health bar hovering around 85%. Nubiri inhaled deeply, her throat glowing a putrid yellow. She turned and roared in Keegan's direction. A cloud of toxin rushed out of her mouth and rolled over him. He coughed and his health bar turned a sickly green, then dropped little by little.

Nubiri pounced into the cloud claws first, but Keegan dodged. Dolli watched his rolling tumble and cast [Gravity Well] where he stopped. The hero resisted her spell and she cursed.

Keegan rushed Dolli, a sanguine aura surrounding him. Ghostly red horns grew from his head and wings sprouted from his back. He lifted off with a flap of his magical wings, dragging his sword across the ground as he flew right over Dolli. She ducked, the blade missing by an inch. Four multicolored lances—one of each Spark alignment—followed him through the air. Two speared him through and dropped his health down to 60%.

Panic rippled through Dolli. They couldn't let him live. They needed the several hours of downtime his respawn would take to rebuild, level up, and prepare themselves.

Keegan yelled as he retreated. "This isn't over!"

"No, it isn't," Nubiri snarled and took off at a run. She flapped her wings hard and lifted into the air twice as fast. Her head darted out on her long neck and snapped down on Keegan's legs. He screamed, twisting and swinging his sword.

Nubiri dropped out of the sky, smashing the buildings below. Dolli and the others dashed through the streets to get to her. Keegan shrieked in pain as Nubiri thrashed her head from side to side. She smashed him through a wall and tossed him into the air, his health bar hanging on by a thread.

He landed in a heap at Nubiri's feet. She whipped her tail around and bashed him into the ground, then picked up his body and threw it into another building. She pumped her wings and jumped, then came down with an earth-trembling thud that cracked the foundation of the buildings around her.

"He's dead!" Dolli screamed, trying to get the enraged wyvern's attention.

Nubiri was laser focused on Keegan's limp body. "Where are my babies?!" The wyvern roared in his face, then whipped him into the street next to Dolli.

The hero rolled to a stop, his legs mangled and one arm missing. His dark plate armor was dented, and blood poured out from the punctures.

Nubiri panted through clenched teeth and pinned Keegan's dead body with a clawed foot. "Answer me!"

The volume of her voice shook the Spark in Dolli's body and vibrated her eyes. Dolli bent down and opened Keegan's loot inventory. He'd dropped a few interesting items, but only one wyvern egg. Dolli pulled the egg out, though it was too heavy for her to carry.

Nubiri dropped low over the egg and gripped it gently in one claw. It was amazing to Dolli how gentle Nubiri could be despite such massive strength.

"Where are the others?" the wyvern snarled at Dolli as if she were hiding them.

Dolli shook her head. "This was the only one he dropped."

"Where are my other two children?" Nubiri barked in Keegan's horror-frozen face.

"He can't tell you. He's dead," Dolli said again and turned the hero's face upward so the wyvern could see. His eyes and mouth were wide open in fear, and blood cascaded down his temples to his neck.

"Where?" Nubiri screamed and flicked her tail, smashing another building.

Dolli ducked as chunks of stone tumbled across the road. "Nubiri, stop!"

The wyvern roared, flicking her tail through buildings as she rampaged down the street. Dolli had no choice. She opened the Overlord menu and selected to return Nubiri to the Lifewell. The wyvern burst in a shower of green sparks and floated up toward Dolli's hut in the woods.

Dolli sighed and dropped to the ground over the egg left behind. She stroked the scaled shell, barely feeling the roughness of it through her hand made of Spark.

"The general store…" Julie said as she picked up a stone painted with blue and red.

"Nubiri just lost two of her babies, I think a few toppled buildings are manageable. We'll have it fixed before nightfall if we work hard," Dolli said, confident in the claim.

Julie threw the rock through Dolli's body. It clattered to the street, pulling a bit of her Spark along with it. Dolli scowled and looked back at the angry woman.

One of the Wispelle crossed his arms. "Didn't hear ya care so much for our lost babies."

Then another spoke up. "You were concerned with the trade reroute!"

"Now our village is falling apart, broken by that *monster*, and you care more for its eggs than our home?" Julie's voice trembled as she spoke.

Heat flared in Dolli that mirrored the feelings of her dungeon-folk. They hated her, and she hated them. How could they think so little of her? She had a thousand different things she wanted to spit back at Julie. A hundred million reasons why they were all wrong. Dolli had cared so much—too much. She'd tried to make their lives perfect! All it took was a little Hero Magic and that had all gone to shit.

"You don't understand," Dolli started.

Julie scoffed. "You're right, I don't. How can you think so little of us? You're supposed to be our ruler!"

"Julie," Rufus said, putting a hand on her smoky shoulder.

Julie pulled away, her body glow dimmed and eyes bright with sadness. "No, Rufus. Even you've said how inept the old witch on the hill was. How you wished Greg would put an end to her! Now we're stuck with her forever!"

The pain was worse than a hundred of Keegan's swords through Dolli's heart. She looked between the accusing Wispelle and her only friend.

"Oh?" Dolli said, her voice threatening to break. Anger, fear, devastation, sickening revolt made her head spin.

"It was a long time ago. We had all been so upset… my boys." There was shame in Rufus' face, but it only hurt her worse.

Dolli nodded, the self-hatred pushing her toward a precipice she couldn't escape. "I understand."

They were quiet for a moment, staring at one another. Dolli activated her corporeal form and picked up the heavy egg.

Dolli turned away for her cottage, unable to face him a second longer. "Do what you will, then."

CHAPTER TWELVE

OLD WITCHES NEVER CHANGE

Dolli sat atop her ruined cabin, a cup of steaming-hot tea beside her. She smiled to herself and took a drink.

Splat.

The liquid passed over her tongue and right through her. It ran down the broken shingles of her home, then pattered against the wood floor. Dolli closed her eyes, took a deep breath, and set the tea aside. The Overlord menu popped open at her command. She found several completed jobs waiting for her, and marked them done, then assigned the dungeonfolk more work.

From her vantage point on top of the dilapidated cottage, Dolli could see the hustle and bustle about the village. They were certainly working hard to fortify the dungeon and make improvements, but Dolli knew it had nothing to do with her inept leadership.

Bitter resentment coursed through Dolli. She crossed her arms and panned over to the Lifewell. Only a few monsters remained in the respawn pool, Nubiri included. She'd been foolish enough to think she could *use* the wyvern's anger to get what she wanted, without being anywhere near high enough level to control the wyvern if something went wrong. The Hero Magic pop-up had told her it would be so, but Dolli was so sure of herself, so confident in her own individual strength, that she couldn't even fathom it to be true.

Inept.

She opened the menu and completed another three quests, then doled out more. An alert popped up in the corner of her vision, a level-up notification. Dolli waved it away and crossed her arms. So what if she was nine. Her presence didn't matter. The people didn't want her. She could just sit in this cabin for the rest of her life, dishing out jobs and leveling for free.

That idea didn't sit well with her, but in honesty, she deserved it.

Inept.

The word felt truer than ever.

Dolli looked down at her feeble hands made of Spark. She couldn't even drink tea anymore… All she was good for was giving out quests and prioritizing respawns, so that's what she'd do. She'd sit up there, do her job, and reap the level rewards she'd earned.

Maybe when Keegan came next, he'd destroy her dungeon core and set them all free.

"Hey." Rufus' voice startled her from the dark thought.

Dolli squared herself, then looked off toward the village. "Is there something you need?"

"I want to apologize."

Dolli's heart thudded, but she kept her calm façade. "That's unnecessary."

Rufus sighed. "Yes, it is necessary. Would you come down?"

She wished she'd selected Wendigo so she could fade into the trees and disappear. Instead, she dropped from the roof and faced the only man she'd thought had been her friend.

"Go ahead then," Dolli said in a monotone voice.

Rufus rolled his black eyes. "Stop being this way! Are you seriously this callous?"

Dolli clapped but only soft puffs of Spark came from her hands. "Best apology I've ever heard."

"This is exactly what I'm talking about! You use this cold sarcasm to hide from what you're feeling. I came to tell you how sorry I was that I'd said that, and how sorry I was for being the coward who couldn't admit it to your face!"

Dolli looked toward the garden, keeping Rufus in her periphery. "Now you've said it and can be on your way."

"That wasn't the whole apology." Cool green moss wrapped around Dolli and turned her toward Rufus. "I'm sorry that I never told you what I said. I'd gotten to know you, and I didn't… I didn't want to ruin our friendship with an ugly thing like that. It was the wrong thing, done for the right reason."

Dolli hummed, then smirked wryly. "The apology was stronger before you tacked an excuse on the end of it."

"You don't take anything seriously, do you?" Rufus said with playful exasperation.

They laughed, and Dolli felt normal for a breath.

A dark realization dawned on her. "I've killed more children."

Rufus scowled. "The eggs?"

"Don't tell me they're just monsters, Rufus. Look at us! *We're monsters!*" Dolli gestured between them, and Rufus only smiled.

"That wasn't what I was going to say, if you'd let me finish."

Dolli crossed her arms and calmed herself.

"They said you didn't care, and I know that's not true. I know how bad it hurt you, and still does. I know you want to be strong and pretend like it doesn't get to you. You'd worked *so* hard for us. I watched our village grow into a city."

He chuckled. "I thought we'd be a kingdom in no time, and I'd be sitting on prime real estate. The boys and I had picked out a nice plot of land in the hills near the lake. They wanted to start farmin' and fishin' to help support the inn. They loved to cook."

Dolli's chest was tight, and her eyes burned with unshed tears. "I took that away from you."

"No, you didn't." He put his hand on her shoulder. "Your actions saved thousands of people. The forty heroes who came through, the ones who made proper potions and got them to the villagers in time, they saved us. That plague would've spread through Little Crossroads like wildfire and reached its black tendrils into the five kingdoms. You could've never produced that number of potions on your own in time, let alone coordinated the quarantine efforts. Rerouting trade saved hundreds of thousands of lives, if not more."

"Yet condemned ours," Dolli said, a lump growing in her throat.

Rufus released her from the [Creeping Moss] and set her down. "You've been lookin' at just one side, Dolli. The ugliest side.

"Maybe that wyvern destroyed some of our home, but it killed Keegan and saved our lives. It provided jobs to help the dungeon-folk level up. You have to look at the bigger picture. There will always be hard choices to make; you can't escape that by tuning us out."

Dolli tutted. "Yeah, you just come screamin' up to my doorstep."

"You know, when you *actually* lead, you lead well." Rufus laid on a bit of guilt with a smile.

"What, you wouldn't prefer Greggy boy?" Dolli taunted.

"I don't know what Julie was on, but I never said *that*." Rufus shook his head.

Dolli paused, the lighthearted moment coming to an end at another realization. "Not that, but you did wish he'd kill me?"

Rufus' smile disappeared. "A deep, dark time ago, I did wish —for a moment—that you were dead."

Dolli's heart ached. She didn't want to be the kind of person who had people wishing for her death, especially not her friend. There was nothing she could do about that thought he'd had. There would always be people out there hating her for what happened, but if she didn't show up, if she didn't try—she would've earned all those thoughts fair and square.

Dolli took a deep breath. "Come inside the cottage."

She turned and wiggled her way into the wide-open living room from the hole in the back wall.

"What are we doing?" Rufus asked.

Dolli brought herself up to her full, tiny height. "Moving."

"What?"

"Well, hiding up in this cottage hasn't been doing any good." She smiled at him over her shoulder, then opened the Dungeon Abilities menu. She selected the Seat of Power [Cottage at the Edge of the Forest] and then selected the Move button. A pop-up appeared with a warning.

[Move Seat of Power]

Moving the Seat of Power can only be done three times per reign. The Core of the dungeon nestled deep beneath the Seat of Power must be removed as well. The Core will need twenty-four hours to reseat in the new location and is more vulnerable in this time.

Are you prepared to move the Seat of Power?
[Yes] [No]

=====

Dolli selected Yes, and another pop-up appeared with Cancel and Place buttons that allowed Dolli to select the location in her zone where she'd like to move the cottage. There was a spot that looked just big enough not too far from the inn, and Dolli thought it appropriate to be closer to the center of town. She'd be part of the action there. Anyone could come to her with anything, and there was nowhere to hide. Perhaps she'd have to build another cottage up in the woods, as she couldn't *always* be the Overlord.

Dolli braced herself, saying, "Hold on to something," then she selected Place.

The ground rumbled and the cottage groaned. Rock cracked and vines snapped as the little hut in the woods lifted from the ground. They rose above the tree line, then drifted lazily toward town. They picked up speed, and when they were well on their way, Dolli wriggled up to a window to watch.

She'd never flown before—despite what they say about witches—and it was enchanting. The glow of dusk, twinkling of stars, blobs of Wispelle down in the village; it was harmonious.

Rufus placed a hand on her shoulder. "Another hard choice down."

CHAPTER THIRTEEN

THE WITCHING HOURS

Dolli shined brightly, using her body like a floodlight while Greg hammered his new contraption into place. It was well into the early morning, and only moments before Dolli knew Keegan would respawn.

"This'ns done," Greg said.

Dolli dropped back and moved out of the way of the trap. Greg pulled the chain and the spring-loaded spiked gate hinged forward from each side of the narrow alley. It clanged shut and locked in place. Greg tugged on the gate firmly, but it held.

The bars were close enough together that most heroes wouldn't be able to slip through like Dolli easily could. She passed through the gate bars, her Spark body oozing around the rough edges of the newly formed metal.

"Do you think it'll be tall enough?" Dolli asked, looking up to the curved hooks that disincentivized climbing over.

Greg shrugged. "Maybe the high Agility heroes'll be able to get over, but the casters, the plate wearers, they'll be trapped."

"That's what we're going for. Good work, Greg." Dolli patted his hand with puffy billows of Spark.

"Thanks… Overlord."

Dolli cringed but kept her comments to herself. She didn't like this "Overlord" nonsense—she was just Dolli—but Rufus said it was good for morale, and whenever they did summon Nubiri again, it would be good for her to know who the dungeonfolk followed.

After an uncomfortable moment of silence, Greg cleared his throat. "So, what's next?"

Dolli opened the Overlord menu and rewarded Greg's completed Alley Traps [8x]. Dolli's body shone brightly, and a rush of energy coursed through her being. A notification appeared in the upper corner of her vision: Level 10.

[Congratulations – You have achieved Level 10]

Congratulations on making it to level 10! Your first Transformation is at hand. Your play style has been analyzed, and two Transformation paths have been selected for your choices.

You will unlock new spells when you select your Transformation.

Unclaimed Stat Points: [10]

Unclaimed Ability Points: [2]

=====

When Dolli closed the pop-up, another appeared with two information cards topped by rotating images of the Wispelle transformations.

The first option looked very much like a Wispelle with a bit more bipedal shape, but the body was a midnight blue that sparkled with glints of gold, red, and pink. It reminded her of the last sliver of a sunset.

[Celestelle – Wispelle Level 10 Transformation]

You've utilized spells that indicate your interest in the greater laws of the universe and the powers from beyond the world of Hafheim.

Transformation Features:

- Increase Magic Affinity for Celestial Aligned Spells by 15%.
- Increase Resistance to Celestial Aligned Spells by 5%.
- Increase Resistance to Divine Aligned Spells by 25%.
- Decrease Magic Affinity for Nature Aligned Spells by 15%.
- Decrease Resistance to Nature Aligned Spells by 15%.
- Gain a free Stat Point in Magic Affinity or Mental Prowess with every level earned.

======

Dolli liked the sound of Celestelle, and the look—though she wouldn't be a good light for working in the dark anymore. The added spell power and bonuses to casting were also attractive—but she would be weaker with Nature magics, like [Mend Wound]. She believed she was set on Celestelle, but wanted to review the other option before she made her choice.

[Ventrelle – Wispelle Level 10 Transformation]

You've been in close combat several times, indicating your desire to bring the fight to your enemy face-to-face.

Transformation Features:

- Ventrelle maintain a solidified form* and can enter vapor form for a cost.
- Increase base Agility, Constitution, Stamina, and Strength by .25x your level.
- Increase Resistance to all Spark Alignments by 15%.
- Decrease Resistance to physical attacks by 50%.

- Decrease Magical Affinity with all Spark Alignments by 50%.
- Gain a free Stat Point in Stamina or Agility with every level earned.

*Upon confirmation, you will select any shape for the Ventrelle that you will maintain.

======

Dolli looked at the rotating blob of a creature. She could mold it to look like herself again—maybe a few years younger, though. Dolli thought of Rufus, the stag-man hybrid, and every other dungeonfolk who would never again look like themselves. How better to set herself apart from them and drive the wedge further?

Reclaiming her former shape was but a fleeting desire. Ventrelle was of no interest to her because of the decreased magical affinity, and she hadn't selected the highest Spark creature just to go back on her plan for magical mastery at level ten.

She selected Celestelle and the pop-up disappeared. The light in the alley faded to a warm orange but was still illuminated quite well.

A new character sheet appeared in her vision. No longer was she a pale-blue vaguely human-shaped blob, but a midnight purple storm, swirling with pink and gold like a nebulous vortex in her chest. The antlers on her head had grown, and little silver star clusters hung between them. The ritual "make-up" on her face had become more intense as well. If it weren't for those light zags on her face, she'd look almost cute instead of horrifying.

Her character sheet aligned with the stat changes of the Celestelle, but she still had some points to distribute. She applied two points each to Magical Affinity, Mental Prowess, Constitution, Stamina, and Agility. She reviewed her changes.

[Dollitrice Grandmeir – Monster Character Sheet]

Name	Level	Alignment
Dollitrice Grandmeir	**10**	**Neutral**
Creature Type	Experience Points	Affiliation
Celestelle	**35**	**Little Crossroads**
Health	Health Regen per sec	Carry Capacity LBS
324	9.22	14.5
Spark	Spark Regen per sec	Movement Speed Bonus
786	24.53	17%
Agility	Constitution	Magical Affinity
9	16	49
Mental Prowess	Stamina	Strength
38	16	3
Melee Damage per sec	Ranged Damage per sec	Spell Damage
5.3	15.8	66.5
Crit Chance	Dodge Chance	Spell Crit Chance
4.75%	7.84%	27.28%
Armor Rating	Armor Piercing	Celestial Res.
9.50%	6.00%	26.78%
Divine Res.	Nature Res.	Nether Res.
31.88%	21.68%	25.50%

=====

"Huh," Greg said with a grunt, pulling Dolli from the menu. She looked up at the scowling man. "What?"

"You're pretty."

Dolli knew Greg didn't mean anything by it. It was more the way one complimented a flower than a potential partner.

She smiled. "Thanks. Now, let's get back to preparations."

They went to the forge and worked on the next round of trap designs with a few apprentice Blacksmiths Greg had been able to conscript with his leveled-up role. Dolli sat off to the side while they worked the bellows and went over her new spell options.

There were four new spells for Celestelle: [Solstorm], [Black-out], [Fold Reality], and [Death Nova]. She reviewed each in turn.

[Celestelle Ability: SOLSTORM]

Spell type: Active

Cost: 80 Spark
Cast time: Channeling
Cooldown: 30 seconds
Duration: 2 seconds per Chain Strike
Range: 5 feet
Target: Any
Spark Alignment: Celestial
Description: Connect the Sol to the natural world through your Spark. From your first target, the Sol will jump at [90]% potency to the next target within 5 feet. This chain will continue until there is no target in range or the spell potency drops to 0%.
Effects:

- When the Sol connects to a Friendly target, they are healed for [10] + 1.2 x your Mental Prowess, modified by the Spell Chain Potency.
- When the Sol connects to a Hostile target, they are dealt [15] +1.5 x your Mental Prowess, modified by the Spell Chain Potency.

======

[Celestelle Ability: BLACKOUT]

Spell type: Active
Cost: 100 Spark
Cast time: Instant
Cooldown: 1 minute
Duration: 5 seconds
Range: 30 feet
Target: Single Hostile
Spark Alignment: Nether
Description: Nighty night...
Effects:

- Render your target unconscious for up to 5 seconds.
- If the target remains unconscious for the duration of the spell, when they awaken they will be debuffed by [Groggy], reducing Mental Prowess by 30% for 90 seconds.

======

[Celestelle Ability: FOLD REALITY]

Spell type: Active
Cost: 100 Spark
Cast time: Instant
Cooldown: 10 minutes
Duration: 10 seconds
Range: 300 feet
Target: Any two points in space not occupied by a living being
Spark Alignment: Celestial
Description: Space is your domain, and you know how to bend the rules. Select any two points in space to be connected as if they were one.
Effects:

- Allow objects and Creatures to pass through each point in space as if they were the same point.
- Neither point can be cast on top of a living being* in a way that would bisect or otherwise trap them in the Fold.

*Disclaimer: Very small and microscopic beings are an exception.

======

[Celestelle Ability: DEATH NOVA]

Spell type: Trigger
Cost: Death's Touch Debuff
Cast time: N/A
Cooldown: 8 Hours
Duration: N/A
Range: 1,000 Feet
Target: Area of Effect
Spark Alignment: Divine
Description: You've made the ultimate sacrifice, now what? Upon death, you send out a burst of Divine Spark in a Nova Wave.
Effects:

- Any Friendly target hit by the Nova Wave will be buffed by Life Boon, healing them for [20] x .5 your Mental Prowess over 10 seconds.
- Any Enemy target hit by the Nova Wave will be debuffed by Spark Rot, draining their Spark Pool by [30] x .5 your Mental Prowess over 20 seconds.
- You will be debuffed by Death's Touch, decreasing your Constitution, Stamina, Strength, and Experience gains by 50% for twenty-four hours.

======

Dolli was stricken with indecision. All of the spells were awesome, so how would she choose?

What helped her dungeon most?

A good question for any leader. [Fold Reality] was a great trump card. She saw endless potential for it, but the cooldown was *so* long, she didn't know if it justified a point, yet. [Death Nova] was a suicide move, which might be useful in the coming battle, but she didn't really want to die, and she *really* didn't want the [Death's Touch] debuff. She'd keep it on the list, but it didn't appear she'd have a choice in the matter if she put a point into that ability. It would always trigger when she died if the cooldown had expired.

[Solstorm] was a definite yes. It matched up perfectly with the corral and trap plan they'd laid out in the dungeon. She dropped one ability point there without a second thought. [Blackout] was another interesting spell she could see being useful, but the fact that it was single target with a long cast time wasn't worth it for the coming battle.

Dolli went back to [Fold Reality]. It had some powerful applications. A thought bloomed in her mind as she looked over the details. There was no limit on how many objects or entities could travel through the opening in the ten seconds it was open.

The wheels of revenge twisted in her mind and Dolli thought of all the ways she could manipulate Keegan with this ability. The look on his face would be priceless. It was too bad Dolli wouldn't see it.

She dropped a point into [Fold Reality], then opened a message to her dungeonfolk: *Minor change of plans. I will be the only bait, and we'll run the heroes through the streets like a maze from the first trap. Come to me in the forge if you have qualms.*

Dolli didn't expect anyone to take issue with only her being the bait. With the plan coming together, Dolli decided to drop one more point in Symbiosis. She would be surrounded by other Wispelle, and would reap deep rewards for the boost. She looked over her spells and abilities one final time.

[Dollitrice Grandmeir – Monster Ability Sheet]

Celestelle Spells and Abilities			
Unclaimed Ability Points: 1	Undiscovered Information	Undiscovered Information	Undiscovered Information
Nature	**Celestial**	**Divine**	**Nether**
Vapor Form (1)	Spark Lance (1)	Zeal (1)	Leech
|	|	|	|
Symbiosis (2)	Starfire (1)	Mend Wounds	Gravity Well (1)
|	|	|	|
Dust Devil<<<<<	Burst of Speed (1)		>>>>>Dust Devil
X /	|	|	|
Solstorm (1)<</	Fold Reality (1)	Death Nova	Blackout
	|	|	|
	?	?	?

=====

With the Overlord menu already open, Dolli saw there were several dungeon quests that had been completed. She went through and marked all of them off. With a flourish of green light, another notification appeared in the corner of her vision. Dolli used to hate the notifications, but now they nearly always meant something great was happening.

She opened the new notification.

[Congratulations – Your dungeon has reached Level 4]

Unused Monster Slots: [44/175]
Undistributed Roles: [3/4]
Open Lifestream Slots: [5/6]
Unclaimed Overlord Ability Points: [2]
[1] levels remain until first dungeon ability: Warmonger; Defender.
[2] levels remain until dungeon renaming is locked.

=====

There was just one level to go and Dolli would be able to turn her band of dungeonfolk into a roving war party to annihilate any and every hero in their path. No more waiting around for heroes to save them. No more waiting around for heroes to kill them. The people of Little Crossroads would revel in their sweet vengeance, and everyone would be happy again.

Everyone but the heroes.

With the dungeon leveling up, two new roles opened. Dolli had one role token to give out, and with the new options so slim —Guardian and Horticulturist—she knew what she had to do. It wasn't going to be a calm return, so Dolli walked to the edge of the forest to summon Nubiri.

The wyvern spun round, looking for an enemy that had only been in her dreams.

"Where is he?" the serpent-like monster asked.

"You killed him," Dolli said.

"Is he not back? Why have you summoned me otherwise?"

Dolli held out a metal badge with a shining shield. "I want you to be the dungeon's Guardian."

The wyvern flapped a wing, batting the pin away. "You want to make me your slave!"

Dolli retrieved the pin from the ground. "You're free to go any time before accepting this role. Everyone here is. But we offer you a safe place to raise your child, whether you want the job or not."

Dolli turned and walked toward the city center.

"Where are my eggs?" Nubiri growled.

Dolli looked back. "One is roosting safely at the seat of power. The other two, I don't know. They weren't on the hero you killed."

"I want them all!" Nubiri roared in Dolli's face, shaking the Spark in her.

"I'm sorry this happened. When Keegan returns, I'll try to get them back. I promise."

"The promise of a human is worthless." Nubiri turned away.

The wyvern trembled, her wings fluttering and fidgeting uncomfortably.

Dolli set the Guardian pin on top of a broken fence post. "I'm a monster now, just like you." Then, she walked away. Nubiri would have to make the best decision for herself, no matter what that was.

"The hero, Keegan, he will return?" Nubiri called after her.

Dolli nodded. "Without a doubt."

Nubiri snarled, her amber eyes shifting back and forth. "You will protect my egg while I fight?"

"With my life." Dolli bowed and touched her forehead, then her heart-center; a solemn promise.

A notification appeared in Dolli's vision alerting her to the advancing presence of heroes from the east—it must've been Keegan. Dolli opened the alert system: *Places, everyone. They've arrived.*

Dolli closed the alert and looked up at the wyvern. "He's here."

Nubiri reached with her claw-tipped wing and grabbed the pin from the fence post. "I can never leave if I accept this?"

"You'll be bound to the dungeon forever, like me."

"Clip my wings and chain my neck," Nubiri said.

"Never. Pull you into the Lifewell before you wreck the whole town, maybe…"

Nubiri growled deep in her throat, a sound like a low chuckle.

"I have to go," Dolli said.

The wyvern looked between the old witch and the pin in her claw. She closed her grip around it, and a notification appeared in Dolli's vision.

[Nubiri Sky-Scar has accepted the role of Guardian!]

The Guardian gains +25% to their base armor when defending the dungeon in addition to new Guardian abilities: [Rallying Call] and [Last Stand]. The Guardian may not take on an apprentice. New Guardian abilities unlock every [5] levels.

=====

Green glowed from Nubiri's palm and the pin shot out of her claw into her chest. The emblem grew two inches in size as it inlaid—seemingly painlessly—into Nubiri's chest. The glowing green faded to a soft hum as it settled in.

"I'll see you on the battlefield." Nubiri flapped her wings, lifting into the air. Dolli watched the wyvern climb into the clouds as she made her way to her position at the east entrance.

The town was quiet, everyone well hidden. Dolli floated past the narrow alley with a hollow floor and a tall gate, then placed the first marker for [Fold Reality]. She continued on to the eastern gate, where she saw Keegan on the other side.

"Upgrades. Nice." Horns grew from his head and the same red wings protruded from his back. "Walls won't stop me," he said, then pulled a glowing stone from his pocket. "It won't stop my friends, either."

CHAPTER FOURTEEN

REUNION MASSACRE

Dolli knew exactly what that stone was, but she wasn't afraid. She'd known Keegan would return with reinforcements—she'd counted on it.

Keegan threw the stone to the ground. It exploded in a blinding flash that made Dolli cover her face. When she opened her eyes, a blue-white portal shimmered below Keegan. A hooded woman in robes of azure silk stepped through carrying a tall glowing staff: Gamergrl12. Then a tall brute with a massive hammer emerged with a wide smile: Jelly-d.

He'd brought the whole murderous gang for a reunion massacre.

More bodies emerged from the portal: a rogue clad in black leather, an archer, a man in opal robes with a wand, on and on until twenty heroes formed a line below the hovering Keegan.

"But wait, that's not all!" Keegan declared.

The azure hero smiled and raised her staff to the sky. Blue-white light shot out from her Spark conduit and ripped a hole in the clouds. Another portal ten times bigger than the first appeared over the outskirts of town. A flying machine unlike anything Dolli had ever seen rippled through into her realm. It was bulbous on top with propellers on each side and had a thick metal under-carriage.

Keegan flapped his wings and came closer, but not so close it was time to [Fold Reality]. He stopped ten feet from Dolli. "I've decided if I can't have my quest reward, there's no reason for you to exist. Last chance, Dollitrice Grandmeir. Give us what we're owed."

Nerves bit at Dolli's insides. Her spell was pulled like a taut rubber band, and the strain was making her arms ache. She had to complete the fold soon. "Like I said, I'd rather die than reward evil like you."

Keegan frowned. "Do it."

The mage—Gamergrl12—cast her staff to the sky again and shot a burst of color over the city. The flying machine whined and accelerated forward across the mountain range. Sparkling spheres dropped from the bottom of the craft and rained down on the place where Dolli's cottage once sat.

Fire erupted into the sky where the orbs fell, and the ground rumbled in anger. A notification blared in Dolli's vision, stating her land was under attack, but she ignored it.

"Time to die, *witch*." Keegan lunged forward and his army charged.

Dolli released the second [Fold Reality] marker an inch from her face and smiled. Keegan, Jelly-d, and two melee blundered through the invisible portal, and Dolli heard pained screams in the streets behind her. Magic bolts and fiery blasts soared toward her, but all vanished right before impact.

Gamergrl12 pointed her staff in anger. "Hacks! Call a GM!"

The spell expired, closing the rift and trapping five of the twenty heroes in the first leg of the maze. Dolli used [Burst of Speed] and zipped back through the narrow slats of the front gate. Sizzling yellow magic blasted against the gates and an arrow pierced Dolli's chest. She winced with pain but wiggled on, getting to the street where the other maze would begin.

Dolli pressed a hand to her chest and looked down at the

faded gold and pink around her midnight blue. Her health bar had dropped by 20% with that single arrow, but she could recover, slowly, if she got out of combat.

Metal clangs and whines came from the eastern gate as the heroes railed against the barrier. She knew it wouldn't hold them —she was counting on that too—but it would slow them down enough for her to get to the next trap.

Monstrous snarls and the sounds of steel on steel rang from one alley over, where Dolli had teleported the first few heroes. She peered around the corner to get a look at the situation.

Keegan was nowhere to be seen. Two heroes lay dead in the pit of spikes, and on the ground next to Jelly-d lay five of Dolli's monsters. The brutish hero swung his warhammer around in an arc and smashed an Osorath in the gut, dropping her health to zero. That was it for Dolli's monsters at this trap. Jelly-d wouldn't be stuck there long, and Dolli had no idea where the rogue character had gone off to.

She hurried back around the corner and sprinted toward another alley. Shouts of "There" and "Get her!" followed. Dolli knew she'd only get away with this trick once, so she had to make it good. She wriggled around another alley and into an open area that had been used as a market.

Another iron fence blocked the path on the other side, and Dolli slipped through. She saw the notification for [Symbiosis] appear in the upper right of her vision and she smirked, then turned and cast [Gravity Well].

Three melee heroes blundered right into the trap, each one slowing to a snail's pace. The casters stayed in the back, out of the area of effect, but that wasn't safe either. Rufus charged in with a group of Stagarth, antlers first. They speared the healers and mages through the chest, then skidded to a halt, launching the screaming, flailing heroes into the center of the [Gravity Well].

But that hadn't been all the heroes. Behind Rufus, Jelly-d and the rogue sliced and smashed their way through. Stagarths with snapped legs and lacerated guts limped from the alley, trying to get away.

"Healers, on the Stags! [Creeping Moss] tanks! Bronzite, shields up! [Starfire] the pit!" Dolli called out commands, but they went unnoticed in the volume of the chaos. They were being overrun, but this was still just a fraction of Dolli's forces. They'd have to fall back to the next trap point.

Dolli had enough Spark and knew she needed to help her troops, so she began the channel for [Solstorm]. Golden light inked out from her chest and burst into the closest monster. Their health bar shot up and their wounds mended themselves in an instant. Then, the gold burst from that monster into the next, and the next, until it reached a hero. It was only at 40% potency at this point, but the resulting explosion of gold fire took a decent 5% health away from the dagger-wielding hero.

"To me, champions!" Keegan's voice boomed over the noise, and the heroes pulled back.

Half of Dolli's dungeonfolk lay wailing in the bloodied street, grasping at their severed limbs and screaming for it all to end. She opened her Overlord menu and quickly pulled all the gravely injured back into the Lifewell once the heroes were out of combat range. They burst in a shower of green and floated up toward the sky, then zipped over to Dolli's cottage at the center of town.

But Keegan and his heroes were leaving… why?

A shadow blotting out the midday sun answered her. Dolli looked up to see the flying machine, orbs poised to drop, sailing toward her cottage. Dolli checked the cooldown on [Fold Reality]; still another five minutes. That thing would be right over her home in half that, and then every citizen of Little Crossroads would be doomed.

Dolli rushed toward her cottage, desperate to do something, *anything* to prevent those explosive orbs from reaching the ground. She cast a [Spark Lance], but the dirigible was out of range. The magic arced, then returned to the earth.

She opened her menu and sent a frantic message: *Any Noctaves, take to the skies and get that thing out of here!*

Within seconds, six black-feathered bodies were racing toward the machine. Blasts of fire and melon-sized projectiles burst from two cannons along the side of the ship. One Noctave went down, and the others circled higher, attacking the balloon. Dolli watched in horror as their attacks did little to deter the ship.

"No, no, no." Dolli wracked her brain for any solution, feeling hopelessness setting in.

A shrill scream pierced the air, and a second, much faster shadow passed overhead. Nubiri dove at the machine, pulling up at the last second and dragging her claws along the unarmored balloon. The material ripped, and hot air hissed as it escaped into the clouds.

The machine listed to the right and warning sirens blared. Little green goblins leapt from the bow. They cast sparkles of blue light at their feet, slowing their decent as the dirigible moaned in complaint. When their little feet touched solid ground, Dolli got a barrage of notifications: all requests to join her dungeon.

Dolli smirked. The hero's own weapons were turning against him.

But there was no time to gloat. Dolli accepted all ten of the requests, and panic returned as she watched the machine fall. The ship was nearly out of the way, but Dolli knew if there were more orbs on board, it could be the end of the entire valley.

Nubiri swooped down and grabbed the metal frame of the machine. The wyvern called to the sky for strength with a burst of yellow light. Wind whooshed through the streets of the village, blowing Dolli along with it. The ship was still sinking, but Nubiri pumped her wings and strained against the inevitable.

The wind slowed, but Nubiri didn't let go of the explosive craft. She pulled and dragged to the very last second when the dirigible crashed into the ground. A fireball engulfed the air above the craft, consuming Nubiri in a torrent of red and orange. The ground shook and a hot blast of air rippled through the streets, but the cottage was safe; Nubiri's baby was safe.

Dolli opened a zone-wide message: *You've fought bravely, my friends! Now, it's time to end this. Converge on X Marks the Spot. We'll make the heroes pay for every inch of ground they think they can take.*

It wasn't the rallying speech she'd hoped for, no crowd of whipped-up citizens to cheer and get their spirits high, but Dolli knew they'd fight hard all the same. They were fighting for their home. They were fighting for each other.

CHAPTER FIFTEEN

BATTLE AT THE CROSSROADS

Dolli raced toward the cottage, using [Burst of Speed] intermittently to get ahead of any of the quick heroes. Within just a few minutes, Dolli had made it to the infamous X for which Rufus had named his inn. She turned and watched her people flood in, some of them wounded, but still ready to fight. These were just farmers, tailors, merchants, and teachers, but they would still fight.

The ten new additions to the dungeon slinked into the square. One goblin, the obvious leader with her fancy hat and handheld telescope, approached Dolli. "Deetu thanks you for sanctuary, Overlord."

"It's a pleasure to have you." Dolli patted Deetu's shoulder, then waved forward the goblins Boji and Moko. It was good to see they were bigger, transformed, and looking healthier than ever.

"Welcome," Boji said.

Deetu smiled and turned to her crew. "Brothers and Sisters, we have found a new port to call home. No more will we slave for the *ty'mak!*"

The goblins raised fists and roared determined cries of freedom.

"The *ty'mak*?" Dolli asked.

Moko grunted. "Mean hero in your tongue. But mean it in very nasty way."

"Very nasty," Boji said with a giggle and a devious smile.

Dolli chuckled, but the cries of her injured people put an end to the jovial moment.

With the goblins introduced, Dolli went on to coordinate healing stations and triage. She knew they wouldn't have much time, but she had to get as many people as possible ready to fight. Those who were too severely injured and obviously in pain, she recalled to the Lifewell.

Julie, her body still the same shape as a Wispelle but now a bright spring green, relieved Dolli with a hand on her shoulder. "I've got it from here. Thank you, Dollitrice."

Dolli paused. "You're welcome."

Julie smiled kindly, then went about her work. The bright green had apparently been an option not offered to Dolli because of her play style, but she assumed it was some healing-oriented transformation. Julie walked the line, using her best heals on the most critically injured. Bones snapped back into place, chunks of missing flesh regrew in an instant, and the wails of the dungeon-folk slowly disappeared.

A red flare in Dolli's vision alerted her to the hero closing in on her turf. There wasn't much time left. She opened her Overlord menu and selected the square as the spawn point for the few dungeonfolk who were healed. Then, she found a set of crates and climbed on top. "They're coming, listen up."

The uninjured dungeonfolk gathered around Dolli, attentive. "Osorath and Bronzite to the front, we need to block the heroes from getting to our casters. Noctaves, take to the skies and draw ranged aggro. Drop boulders, sticks, bodies, whatever you have to. Keep their attention off our frontline warriors.

"Damage Wispelle, primarily use the area of effect spells on mid- to back-row clusters. Save your [Spark Lance] for low health tanks up front. Keep [Gravity Well] active at the front at all times.

Healing Wispelle, stand forty feet behind your tank. If they fall, support the next closest tank or melee damage dealer."

The group was nodding agreement, and though Dolli was scared, she felt hopeful. "Wendigos, watch the flanks. Stay back and stealthed until you have a mark. They will try to sneak around the sides to get our healers. And everyone… try to stay alive."

"You too," Greg said from the back of the crowd.

Dolli's chest swelled, not just with hope for the coming battle, but for the coming years. She grinned. "Let's kill some heroes."

The dungeonfolk cheered with fists raised and heads held high.

"Dollitrice!" Keegan screamed above the roar of the crowd, and they fell quiet.

The tanks moved to the outside of the ring and the Wispelle clustered toward Dolli. More heroes appeared at the alleyways and on top of buildings behind Keegan.

He pointed a red-glowing arm at the burning wreckage on the outskirts of town. "That was an ultra-rare zeppelin!"

"Don't worry, the goblins made it out fine," Dolli said. She gestured to the pack of green-skinned monsters. They cracked their knuckles, grins revealing sharpened teeth.

"You stole my goblins?!" Keegan's voice broke and the air around his body glowed bright red. Dolli'd seen this one enough times.

Before Keegan darted forward, Dolli was already dodging. He sailed through the air, unable to change his course, and smashed into the wall. The dungeonfolk scattered away from him, but the heroes around the outside charged.

"Remember the plan!" Dolli screamed, and the chaos organized. Tanks rushed forward, and Wispelle followed not far behind, casting green showers over the Bronzite and Belgruses. Wendigo guarded their Wispelle's flanks, and the five remaining Noctaves took to the sky.

"Why won't you just do what I want?" Keegan screamed and tore after Dolli.

She dropped a [Gravity Well] behind her and weaved through the crowd. The dungeonfolk were executing the plan, but the heroes were still so strong. Dolli used [Burst of Speed] and slipped through the clash, casting a quick [Starfire] over the hero healers in the back.

The casters ran in all directions, breaking ranks, and arrows sailed toward Dolli. She fell back into the front line, slipping between clashing swords and claws. Suddenly, a notification appeared in the corner of her vision. The dungeon had leveled up!

"Where are you, *witch?*" Keegan boomed from overhead, his wings casting red ripples across the battlefield.

Dolli opened the Overlord menu to the first Transformation screen. [Warmongers] stared her in the face… but Dolli's people wouldn't survive this fight if she picked it. She swallowed her black desire for revenge and selected [Defenders].

Another pop-up consumed her vision an instant later but she didn't have time to read.

"I see you!" Keegan said.

She couldn't close the menu, so she ran blind while she scanned the screen. There were two buttons at the bottom: [Ascend] and [Descend]. Dolli quickly pieced together the meaning of the frantically picked-out words. Her dungeon would grow up, or down. High ground was always better.

Still running blind, Dolli selected [Ascend].

The ground trembled and shifted and the sounds of battle slowed. A rumble deep in the earth boomed; then, the ground began to rise. Dolli finally closed the menu and saw where she was going: straight toward the cottage. Damn her instincts.

"So, this is where you hid it!" Keegan said with delight as he soared past Dolli.

Jelly-d emerged from an alley at the edge of the cottage, his hammer smeared with her monsters' blood. He eyed the egg in its carved-out pumpkin roost.

"Don't you dare touch that!" Dolli yelled, pointing at Jelly-d.

Keegan raised his sword overhead and the sky around them darkened. "Give me my quest reward, Dollitrice, or your reign ends forever."

Jelly-d raised his orange glowing hammer overhead, a murderous glint in his eye. Dolli looked between Keegan and Jelly-d, faced with yet another difficult choice. Save herself and her people, or uphold her promise to Nubiri.

"Last chance!" Keegan declared.

"Okay!" Dolli said. "Where are Nubiri's eggs, the other two? If you give them to me, I'll complete the quest."

Keegan scowled. "You've been holding out for *years* and now you'll give it up for a couple of wyvern eggs? I sold them on the auction already, so… I guess I'm never getting that quest completed." Red lightning spiked out from the tip of Keegan's sword and zapped the ground near Dolli, blasting her backward three feet.

Jelly-d swung his hammer and Dolli held her breath. No. This couldn't be the only way. This couldn't be how it ended for them. She watched at the apex of a gasp, begging for a solution that would let her win. *For once, please, just let me save them all!*

There, at the crossroad of desperation and despair, Dolli was struck with inspiration. She threw out her hand, placing the mark for [Fold Reality] over Nubiri's egg, then looked to Keegan and dropped the other at an angle over the back of his head.

In a deafening crack of orange, Jelly-d's hammer smashed into Keegan's spine. Keegan soared forward, a hole blasted in his chest. The hero landed with a heavy thud at Dolli's side, and his sword clattered to the ground. The red glow faded from the metal, and Keegan's eyes went distant.

"Sorry, Kee!" Jelly-d said, though it was obvious Keegan was dead and could not hear him. Jelly-d winced as if he were being scolded, and then his gaze settled on Dolli. "Can do, big hoss."

The brute hiked his hammer up his shoulder and smiled at Dolli. "You've used up all your bag of tricks."

Dolli checked the Lifewell and smirked. "Not yet." She

selected the fully healed skolf and spawned them right next to her.

Jelly-d laughed. "Those things? I used to kill those back in my starting zone."

"Eat!" Dolli declared, and the skolf darted forward.

Jelly-d smashed at the ground, but the skolf were too fast. They darted around his attacks and found the little holes in his armor, slipping inside.

Jelly-d screamed and flailed, his health dropping in slow, nibbling bites. Then, in a fit of madness, he beat his hammer against his chest, dealing a hefty 10% damage to himself. There was a sad squelch and the brute beat his chest again in defiance.

He pinned Dolli with a furious glare. "Ouch."

The rumbling, rising ground finally came to a stop and Jelly-d lost his footing. Dolli went to cast [Spark Lance], but a negative buzz blared in her ear, letting her know she was dry. She really was out of tricks. The best she could do was try to push him over, but even then, she weighed nothing.

Jelly-d scrunched up his face, then leaned to the side and vomited. He pulled at his breastplate, ripping it free after fumbling for a second. The two dead skolf fell to the ground with the clatter of metal, and a pungent stink wafted toward Dolli. Even in death, her monsters fought for her.

She charged forward, unsure of what she would do, or what she *could* do. Die for her people if she had to. Before she reached the retching hero, a towering wall of stone stepped between them.

Greg, with his blacksmith's hammer in one hand and a sheet of metal in the other, bellowed a war cry. "Don't come back now, ya hear?"

He pulled back on the hammer and swung it into Jelly-d's face with all his might. Dolli looked away but heard the telltale crack of a skull and thud of a body against the paved street.

The heroes disintegrated into sparkles of gold, heading off toward their respawn point and leaving behind precious loot.

Dolli opened her Overlord menu to see not a single blotch of red on her zone map.

It was finally over. The heroes were gone.

CHAPTER SIXTEEN

NO REST FOR THE WITCHES

In a blur of color and sound, Dolli respawned next to her cottage at the center of the village. The sun had fallen below the horizon, but the ember glows of the burning zeppelin kept the city in perpetual twilight. Dolli's [Exhaustion] debuff was pushed back another twenty-four hours from her four-hour rest, which had passed in the blink of an eye.

She took one deep breath, coughed from the smoke of the fire, then got to work. Nearly every quest she'd given out had been completed, and yet her people hadn't stopped working. Experience points or no, they had to get the town back in order.

"There you are," Julie said when she noticed Dolli.

"Anything interesting happen during my slumber?" Dolli asked.

Julie shook her head. "Quiet as the grave." She chuckled. "The apprentice Blacksmiths have repaired much of the fencing, but with our new *elevated* status, I was thinking…"

"Let's hear it," Dolli said with a nod.

"The whole village has risen by fifteen feet. That's not quite enough to do anything with now, but I'm guessing it's not done growing."

Dolli opened the Overlord menu and looked at the Dungeon

Path. Sure enough, with every new level they gained, the dungeon would ascend another increment—which increased over time.

"You're correct in your assumption."

"Excellent! My thought is instead of build'n gates and traps all over the city, we could keep it nice, build homes for the folk, and let the heroes run around in the mazes below us. We could dig down, create an openin' for them. If they wanted to come claim our riches, or your seat, they'd have to traverse the maze of traps. We'd go down and patrol of course, killin' and stealin' from 'em."

Dolli didn't close her menu while she listened. Instead, she panned over to the Roles section and looked at the level 1 role she'd thought useless: Architect.

"Julie, how would you like a role?" Dolli asked, pulling the pin from the ether into her hand.

Julie shrugged. "Never was much for breads, but seein' as I don't need to eat anymore..."

Dolli cocked her head and held out the pin.

"Oh! You mean a title!" Julie reached out for the little bit of metal in Dolli's hand. She inspected it for a moment, then grimaced. "I don't know if I'm the right person."

Dolli looked around the village. "You cared for the church all these years, kept it nice."

"That was different. It's just one building—and I'm not tellin' people how to build it, just keepin' it in good condition."

Dolli hummed. "You seem to have this grand vision for how to use the space below us. I think you're not giving yourself enough credit, or opportunity for growth."

"But what if I mess up?"

"Of course you will," Dolli said. "That's just part of it."

Julie's eyes widened. "What if I collapse the whole village?!"

Dolli shrugged. "Then we'll have a lot of quests to fix it back up—more experience for everyone, and the dungeon. But maybe you should practice in an area near the outskirts..."

"Yes, that would be best. Smaller mistakes, smaller messes."

[Julie Harken has accepted the role of Architect!]

"You have the power to give out your own quests now related to anything you want to build. There's starting to be a few people here who can give out quests…" Dolli stroked her chin while she thought. Dolli and anyone else with a role would need resources and assistants, and there were only so many dungeonfolk—for now. The best way to keep everything running smoothly would be to work together.

"I'll speak with the others, and we can set up a teatime to review our plans, prioritize where we send help, and create a rotation for returning to the Lifewell to prevent exhaustion."

"I'll chat about that with Greg on my way out, if you'd like," Julie said.

"When the sun rises, meet back at the cottage. Thank you, Julie."

The woman turned Wispelle beamed. "You're very welcome, Overlord."

Dolli stopped by Nubiri's egg before leaving. She put her midnight blue hand on the warm shell, stroking it gently. "You're safe, little one. Mother will be back soon, but we're all here to protect you."

The Wendigo child ran past the cottage, chased by his Wispelle friend. Dolli felt the squeezing pressure of guilt compressing her chest, but then, they giggled. They frolicked and floated, delighting in the abilities of their new forms. It wouldn't be a normal childhood—not after what they'd seen—but perhaps it could still be a good one. A fulfilled one.

Dolli made a note to make sure the children's mental states were well, and to observe them to ensure they aged. It would be a horrible circumstance to be trapped as a child forever. Dolli still wasn't certain how any of this dungeon and monster stuff worked. They didn't eat or sleep, they respawned like heroes, and they transformed every ten levels. What if they never grew old?

What if they grew old very quickly? If they died of old age, would they respawn?

She felt she had too many questions and too few answers.

Answers would come with time. For now, she had to focus on the next step for survival. There were still two role slots she could fill since she hadn't given one out at Dungeon level 4. The more dungeonfolk she had specializing in certain areas and able to give out quests, the better. She would lean on leaders to know what was best for their area of expertise and help them all come to agreement on daily division of labor over tea.

The roles remaining were Lieutenant—one of the roles she'd had since level 1 that she could not award to herself—Alchemist, Horticulturist, and Tinkerer. She knew exactly where to go next.

Dolli walked around the corner to X Marks the Spot to find Rufus working in the light of a torch. He hammered a board into place to patch a gaping hole made from the battle.

"Ho' there," Dolli said in a deep, playful tone that mocked Greg. "How's this coming? Using enough nails?"

"Too many, apparently," Rufus said, then rolled his eyes at Dolli.

She laughed. "We've got enough spare metal; I think we'll be fine."

"Well, what brings you all the way down here?" Rufus set his hammer aside and pulled up a barrel to sit on.

Dolli opened the Overlord menu and summoned the Lieutenant pin into her hand. "I want you to be my right hand. When I'm dead, or in the Lifewell resting, I want you to be in charge. The dungeonfolk respect you, and your combat coordination is good. You have your finger on the pulse of the village, and you're the centerpiece here. Information flows to you at the inn, or I suspect it will again when you get a good brew on tap."

They shared a laugh, then Rufus reached out for the pin.

"I'm honored," he said, inspecting it. "Are you sure this is the right choice? What about Brene?"

"Brene is a good soldier. I'm sure there will be a role for her in the future, but this one is for you."

"But why me?"

Dolli scowled. "Were the reasons I offered not good enough? I could come up with more. Let's see, you've been loyal, supportive, my only friend…"

Rufus shook his head and smiled. "I just wonder if there isn't someone better. Someone more—"

"There isn't anyone better, or more," Dolli said. "If you don't want it now, it'll be here when you do."

Rufus pulled in a deep breath, then a pop-up appeared in Dolli's vision.

[Rufus Kruger has accepted the role of Lieutenant!]

"I know that's a lot of responsibility. Thank you," Dolli said.

"You're welcome," Rufus replied with a smile.

Dolli turned to head back home, then paused. "Teatime is at dawn in my cottage. We'll discuss allocation of resources and labor, breaks and Lifewell rotations, plans, the like. Everyone with a role will be there."

Rufus grunted. "Meetings. I didn't sign up for any meetings."

"Read the fine print next time!" Dolli gave him a wave and headed off.

She returned to the cottage and sat in the rocking chair, then reviewed the roles again. The smartest choice for Alchemist would certainly be Dolli. No one knew local fauna like she did, but could she give herself a role?

She grabbed the pin and held it out, then focused on it. A pop-up appeared.

[Would you like to take on the role of Alchemist?]

The Dungeon Alchemist oversees keeping the battle potions stocked and poisons flowing. Increased natural essence affinity by

15%, decreasing the likelihood of damaging plant ingredients during all processes. Your potions book will be available in your menu, and with every level gained, new innate recipes unlock. You may add potions to your recipe book from other sources such as alchemists' records, scrolls, and more.

You may take on a single apprentice at level [5].

Overlord Bonus Perk: Every two hours you may spawn simple ingredients or tools in your designated workshop for the cost of 100 Spark.

Would you like to claim this role? [YES] [NO]

======

By the gods, she could. And she got a bonus for being the Overlord. Dolli accepted and glanced up to the top of the bookshelf where her recipe books sat. There was still more to do in the menus, though, so Dolli returned to completing quests and assigning new ones.

There were intermittent requests from random monsters asking to join the dungeon, all of which Dolli approved. She'd have to coordinate some kind of "Welcome" meeting. Or perhaps she could get Rufus to do that…

Dolli saw the Hero Quests menu floating aimlessly amid the sea of Overlord tabs. She opened it to see the Plague quest staring back at her, and one hero name on the active list: Keegan. Dolli had hoped she'd never have to see him again, but it looked as though he was going to be just as stubborn as she could be.

She welcomed the challenge. She invited the threat that pushed her and her dungeonfolk to greatness. Let him come. They would be ready.

The night passed all too fast. As the sun touched the treetops to the east, Greg, Julie, and Rufus gathered at the cottage, and Dolli made a pot of tea. Nubiri was still in the Lifestream, but Dolli would fill her in on all the happenings.

"First order of business," Dolli said, starting the gathering.

"We need to name our dungeon. If we level up again, we will forever be known as the Dungeon of Little Crossroads."

"That dudn't have a very nice ring," Greg said.

"No," Julie agreed.

"How about Monstrocity, like Monster City. We're all monsters, and Dolli, you've been getting new recruits by the hour," Rufus said.

"Hmm, not bad. What about Monstropolis?" Dolli offered.

The group mumbled and shook their heads.

Julie scowled. "You've got it all wrong. Dollitrice, from the moment we became a dungeon you've been lettin' monsters in from all walks—this is true. But we're not a monster city, and we're not Little Crossroads anymore. We're a haven for those who've escaped the heroes' murderous reach."

"Haven…" Dolli tried on the word.

"Monster Haven?" Rufus said.

Julie growled. "What's with you and this monster business?"

"Monster Haven," Greg repeated with an approving nod.

"I like it," Dolli said. "Julie? We have to vote unanimously."

Julie rolled her eyes. "Yeah, it's not a bad name, really…"

"It's settled then." Dolli opened the menu and input the name, claiming their new identity.

Dolli closed the menu and looked around at her people. What did the future hold for Monster Haven? She was sure they'd discover it together, but Dolli knew there'd be no small amount of hero murder to go around. They needed to be ready, all of them.

Dolli cleared her throat. "Next order of business; combat training."

THE END
Reluctant Dungeon
Monster Haven Book 1

REVENGING DUNGEON

J.D. ASTRA

MONSTER HAVEN BOOK TWO

THE ADVENTURE CONTINUES...

… in *Revenging Dungeon (Monster Haven Book 2).*

Can Dolli's poisonous past save her from a dungeon eater?

Dolli was just getting to like the idea of being the overlord of Monster Haven when a roaming Warmonger set his eyes on her dungeon core. Some of her citizens have defected to the enemy horde for the promise of safety, and now Dolli has a choice to make. Does she wipe them out to save those who remain, or does she sacrifice herself to save them all?

But the defectors don't know that the Warmonger has an even more sinister plot than just consuming Dolli's core—and when they finally see his true monstrous nature, will it be too late? Dolli needs a killer cure, a poison so toxic it might wreck her and the enemy. She needs... a Hero.

BOOKS AND REVIEWS

If you loved *Reluctant Dungeon* and would like stay in the loop about the latest book releases, deals, and giveaways, be sure to subscribe to the Shadow Alley Press Mailing List.

www.ShadowAlleyPress.com

Sign up now and get a free copy of our bestselling anthology, Viridian Gate Online: Side Quests! Your email address will never be shared and you can unsubscribe at any time.

Word-of-mouth and book reviews are beyond helpful for the success of any writer, so please consider leaving a rating or a short, honest review on Amazon—just a couple of lines about your overall reading experience. Thank you in advance!

You can also connect with us on our Facebook Page where we do even more giveaways: facebook.com/shadowalleypress

BOOKS BY SHADOW ALLEY PRESS

ENTER THE SHADOW ALLEY LIBRARY to take a peek at all of our amazing Gamelit, Fantasy, and Science Fiction books! Viridian Gate Online, Rogue Dungeon, Snake's Life, Dungeon Heart, Path of the Thunderbird, School of Swords and Serpents, the FiveFold Universe, and so many more... Your next favorite book is waiting for you inside!

A WORD FROM (JESS) J.D. ASTRA!

Henlo there my dudes! I hope you enjoyed the read, and really look forward to seeing your thoughts online! Come hang out in my discord server:

https://discord.gg/ZRSSvgRh6k

Not a fan of Discord? Follow me on Facebook for memes and updates here:

https://www.facebook.com/theastralscribe

If Facebook isn't your thing, you can sign up for my mailing list for a free novella set in the Bastion Academy series, and get monthly updates here:

http://subscribe.astralscribe.com/bastionsubs

If you're looking to support me (<3 thank you!) and get super exclusive access to early chapters, arts, special updates, and more, you can find me on Patreon here:

https://www.patreon.com/jdastra

Here's some of those awesome Patrons, my Friendly Townsfolk+:

Tyler O. | eden H. | Janet S. | Joseph O. | Ken R. | Laura L. | Remy J. | Ray Allen | Daniel M.

STILL not seeing your jam? These things receive less love, but…

I have a website: www.astralscribe.com

You can email me directly: contact@astralscribe.com

TikTok: @jd_astra

ABOUT THE AUTHOR

About me... I'm a baller. Keyboard crawler. 20 inch display, on my ink scrawler. Holler. Getting flayed tonight, all my characters getting splayed tonight!

In my spare time I love to cook, hike, play video games, and spend quality time with my people.

Three questions people never ask me are; how do I look at myself in the mirror, what's in the box, and what does it take to build a story with likable characters in an interesting setting with important goals?

The answer to the last is determination, dedication, and sacrifice. I've been working at being a writer since before I could string more than two sentences together, and it never gets easier, but it does get better.

I'm surrounded by people who love and support me, which is the most amazing gift the universe could ever give. I will never give up, never surrender, and hopefully, keep on entertaining for the rest of my life.

9 798836 256487